HUNTED

A JT THOMAS NOVEL

E. A. Fleischauer

FIRST EDITION SEPTEMBER 2019

Copyright 2019 by E. Alan Fleischauer

ISBN-13: 978-1-7335940-1-1

HUNTED

Chapter One

John Thurgood Thomas was happy to be back in Colorado. Traveling to New York had made him rich, but it also cost him the love of his life. His fiancée Annabelle had been gunned down by her estranged husband in cold blood, and JT knew that he would never find another like her. He thought about her as soon as he woke, when he lay down to sleep, and countless times in between.

The good news was that Annabelle had a wonderful, talented daughter who was planning to visit once her school term was over. Maddy had a terrible relationship with her father, but JT had become very protective of her. He hoped he could fill a little bit of the void left behind by her dad.

JT had ridden the train back with Gregor Nelson. Gregor was an investigator for a New York law firm, a former federal marshal, and a Pinkerton agent. JT had hired him to file a claim on the cave he had discovered near Point Stevens Pass, Colorado. It had yielded a hoard of valuables, and JT needed him to secure its remaining contents.

With the help of some workers, Gregor had tarped the ornate furniture and moved everything into a local warehouse. These men worked under the cover of darkness and were paid a modest amount and to complete the task before moving on to their next destination. Emma, owner of the local boarding house, was tasked with keeping an eye on the items and making sure they were left unopened.

When news of JT and Annabelle's plight reached him, Gregor halted his mission and returned to New York. Now he was looking forward to reconnecting with Emma, whom he had taken a liking to.

JT was looking forward to unsealing the beautiful chests, hutches, and armoires from the cave. There, Annabelle had discovered the "Crown Jewels"'" inside an ornate desk, and their sale at a New York auction had provided JT with enough money to last him the rest of his life. But with Annabelle gone, JT needed a purpose in life, and the intrigue of remaining treasure was beckoning him back to Colorado. He knew that Annabelle would have wanted him to search the remainder of the drawers and cubbyholes; in fact, she would have led the charge.

After getting off the train and returning to Point Stevens Pass, he suddenly felt uneasy about reconnecting with his new friends. The familiar scene was a keen reminder of Annabelle's absence. He simply wanted to pick up his horses and head out to his cabin in the mountains.

He stopped first at the mercantile to stock up, then headed to Buck's Livery. The stable was unmanned, but his horses were there and he greeted them like family. A minute later, Buck walked in.

"Hello," Buck said. "Long time no see!"

JT chuckled. "Yeah, it's been a while. Good to see you. Looks like you took good care of my horses!"

"Well, you said to take care of them like family and I did. They are fine animals and I'd be glad to buy them from you," Buck replied.

JT nodded. "Well, you would have to get in line. I'm not parting with them in any case, but thanks for filling in for me and taking good care of them." He pitched Buck a twenty-dollar gold coin.

Buck looked at it, bit it, and looked up at JT. "Hey, you paid me enough before you left."

JT laughed. "Well, things have changed and you deserve it. I'm headed out to my cabin for a month or two. Would you save a spot for Pete and Re-Pete?"

"You bet," Buck said, as he began saddling the horses.

JT loaded his saddlebags and scabbards. "Tell Emma and Gregor where I went and to guard my cave interests until I get back." He pitched Buck another ten-dollar gold piece.

Buck caught the coin and smiled. "Yes sir, I will. And safe travels, Mr. JT."

$$\approx \approx \approx \approx \approx$$

JT took a leisurely ride to his cabin. He camped where he wanted, sometimes cutting the days short. He had missed his horses, and it seemed as though they were enjoying the trip as much as he was. Pete and Re-Pete were long horses, relishing in long strides and long-distance gallops. When they camped for the night, they pawed the ground and shook their heads, acknowledging the pleasures of the day.

As JT neared his cabin, he pulled out his long glass and was surprised to see three horses tied to his hitching rail. They were saddled, but the riders were nowhere to be seen. His cabin was remote and he really didn't have any neighbors, so he moved his horses back into the forest and dismounted. He patted Pete and Re-Pete while tying them loosely to a large oak tree. "You boys stay here; I'll be back in a bit," he whispered.

JT made his way to the windowless back of the cabin, then under the front deck, listening for any movement. Hearing nothing, he slipped the hammer strap off his father's Colt while taking off his Stetson. He quietly made his way up the deck steps, keeping low enough to not be seen through the windows. He worked his way to the side of the cabin and peeked in the window.

Inside were three scruffy hombres sitting around his kitchen table, drinking his whiskey and playing cards. He did not recognize any of them, but they sure didn't look like fine, upstanding citizens. JT squatted down and made his way to the front door. He drew his Colt, quietly turned the doorknob, and stepped into his cabin. Two of the card players jumped up, trying to remove the hammer straps from their six-guns. "It's him, let's take him!" the stranger on the left shouted, as he removed his revolver from its holster.

JT quickly fanned a shot from his Colt into the man's chest, sending fire, smoke, and death. The man crumpled to the floor. The other man who was standing pulled back on his revolver's hammer, but JT took careful aim and put a well-placed shot into his heart. The third card player slowly stood up with an evil look on his face. "You killed my friends, you son of a bitch," he growled as he drew his Colt. JT shook his head and fanned two shots into the man's gut. He collapsed into the chair, dropping his weapon and grabbing his stomach. Looking up at JT, he quietly whispered, "So close, so close to $10,000," as he died.

JT kept the man covered, making sure he was dead before taking the gun out of his hand. He checked the other two strangers, dead and bleeding on his hardwood floor. He shook his head, thinking *$10,000? What $10,000?*

Weeks passed at the cabin. JT had washed the blood off his newly refinished floor before it could stain, having learned his lesson the last time this happened. He welcomed the three new horses into his stable, their former owners now in a shallow grave a few hundred yards away. He woke up when he wanted, did some hunting with his Greener shotgun and Winchester rifle, fished, cooked, and practiced daily with the dueling pistol from the cave.

The combination of the cut-down holster and the unique handgun was something that he had never experienced before. The gun nearly jumped out of the holster, and with the large hammer, he was able to fan it and hit four cans in the blink of an eye. He thought about replacing his father's Colt with the "cave gun" as he now called it, but decided against it. His father's Colt held much sentimental value.

As he worked on the cabin he thought constantly about Annabelle, and actually talked to her while making repairs. He asked her advice on tough jobs and imagined how she would like things to look, then proceeded as she would have liked. It was comforting and sad at the same time. JT knew he could never find another like her.

By the end of the fifth week, JT had run out of things to repair. After washing the blood off his prized hardwood floor, he found some old but serviceable sandpaper and sanded the spots until no stains were left. He had a bit of shellac left over from when he installed the floor, but because it had been through a cold freezing winter, he decided to get more from the mercantile. He was running out of staples too, so early the next morning he packed up, readied his horses, and headed for Point Stevens Pass. The journey under the late-October sky was magnificent, with the leaves changing, the chilly nights, and the scent of the coming winter on the breeze.

Chapter Two

JT arrived in town at dusk and headed directly to the livery. Buck was there, soaping a saddle. "Well, Mr. JT," he exclaimed, "where did you get all these horses?"

JT smiled and replied, "Oh, the owners don't need them in hell, so I thought I'd bring them here and see if you wanted them."

Buck looked them over and nodded. "Sure, I can buy them from you. They aren't anything near Pete and Re-Pete, but they will do in a pinch!"

"Naw, they're yours. I have no use for them."

Buck smiled. "I'll tell you what. How about I give one to my young helper Drew? He is a good kid, a hard worker, and he doesn't have a horse."

"That would be fine, and give him the saddle as well. You keep the Winchester and the Sharps though," JT said, pointing to the scabbards on the new horses. "I cleaned and oiled them and they are in pretty good shape."

"Well thank you kindly, Mr. JT. You surely are a generous guy!"

"My pleasure," JT replied, as he headed to the hotel.

After checking in and noting that Gregor and Emma were still in residence, he left a note with the reception clerk asking if they would join him for breakfast.

≈ ≈ ≈ ≈ ≈

Gregor and Emma were already at the table when JT arrived. He smiled when he saw they were obviously smitten with each other. In his estimation they deserved some happiness, and seeing them smiling and joking did his spirit good. Emma stood up and gave JT a hug, and Gregor gave him a firm handshake.

Emma looked at JT after they had ordered. "I am so sorry about Annabelle. Gregor told me all about it," she stated quietly.

JT nodded. "I miss her. We were going to get married and now I'm just trying to come to terms with it all," he said with a shrug.

"Well she was a wonderful lady," Gregor said, "but I'm sure she would want you to carry on."

"Oh absolutely!" Emma exclaimed. "You know she was anxious to see what was inside the rest of the cave furniture. We brought it all back here to Point Stevens Pass and it is stored in a warehouse across from the livery.

JT looked up. "Well, Annabelle was always up for an adventure!" he said.

"That's right!" Emma said with a smile.

"Well, are you ready to find another Crown Jewel necklace or another bag of diamonds?" JT asked, standing up and chuckling.

Emma looked up and smiled. "Why not? Who knows what is in those cubbies and drawers?"

Gregor added, "Well, let's eat and get over there. I've been wondering about this since you hired me, JT. And by the way, the claims are all filed and you are now the sole legal owner of the cave and its contents."

"That's a relief!" JT said, grinning.

The trio hurried through their meal and walked briskly toward the warehouse. As they passed the quickly rising boarding house that Emma owned, she waved at the workers and touched JT's elbow gently.

"Thank you again for the money to rebuild, JT. It is going to be larger and have a small café, both for the boarders and the public. Also, my room is going to have a larger bed," she said, winking at Gregor. "There also will be a suite called the JT Thomas suite. For you sir, there will be no charge!"

JT smiled while Gregor blushed. "That's very nice of you! I'm sure it will be beautiful," he said.

Emma nodded. "And quite a few pieces that you are generously giving me from the cave will be in your suite as well! I have already decorated it in my mind."

Gregor unlocked the warehouse door, relocking it after they entered. He and Emma pulled the shades to let the sunshine in while JT stood back and surveyed the furniture pieces.

"Well, there is more here than I expected," he said, pulling a cover off the nearest piece. "Is this all of it?"

"Most of it," Gregor said. "Some pieces were already damaged and are only good for kindling. The good pieces were spread out quite a ways along the cave wall. We were careful moving them; some of these are probably worth a small fortune on their own. The original owners sure had good taste!"

Gregor put a hand on JT's shoulder. "But listen, JT. Once we emptied it out, I had my mine expert examine the cave, and he saw gold veins in the walls. He is back in Golden, but he said he would leave a rock drill and a bunch of dynamite at the entrance of the cave. He and his crew are available if you want them to do the blasting, or as he put it, "Have at it if you want but be careful with that damn dynamite!"

JT laughed. "The cave that keeps giving! But let's not worry about blasting today."

"Then shall we get started?" Emma asked. "JT, you start on that end, Gregor will be on the other end, and I'll start in the middle. If you find anything of interest holler out!"

"Yes, ma'am!" JT and Gregor said in unison.

After nearly an hour no one had discovered anything of value. Then Emma removed a cover from a bedroom chest and opened the top drawer to find women's blouses. She slid the drawer out and slowly removed the items one at a time, fully expecting to find more diamonds. As she got to the bottom of the stack, she squealed and dropped the drawer, spilling the remaining contents. As it hit the floor, a mouse jumped out and scurried off into the dark corners of the warehouse. "I hate mice!" Emma exclaimed, as JT and Gregor laughed.

"Well, if it's any consolation I do too," said JT.

Emma looked down at the exposed bottom of the drawer. There was something that looked like a folded map inside. "Hmm," she said, as she removed it and held it up. "Look what I found!"

She moved over to the desk where Annabelle had found the Crown Jewel necklace and spread the map out on the desk. JT and Gregor hurried over to take a look. The document was divided into three sections, one of which depicted a small part of Nevada and California with a highlight on a town called Truckee.

JT pointed at the written section. "That's not English," he stated.

"No, it surely isn't," Gregor agreed. "That's Chinese, I'm thinking."

"Can you read it?" Emma asked.

"Heck, no. I just recognize it from my time as a Federal Marshal. Our cleaning folks were Chinese and would leave each other notes and it sure looked like this!"

JT nodded. "Well, the main portion of the map seems pretty detailed. There is even a mileage scale in the corner. And look at the spot marked with an X, just outside of Truckee, California."

"I wonder how far it is?" Emma inquired.

"Good question. I wish we had a ruler," JT replied.

Emma pulled up the desk chair and opened a slim drawer located underneath the lip of the desk. The drawer was full of pencils but a ruler was not visible. She moved the pencils out of the way and put her head down to see what was behind them. She stuck her hand in and groped around a bit, trying to get a grip on something.

"What'cha got there?" Gregor chuckled. "Another mouse?"

Emma grunted as she withdrew a small purple velvet bag and laid it gingerly on the desk. "I don't think it's a mouse," she said with a grin, "but I sure recognize that color. Don't you, JT?"

JT nodded. "Oh yes," he said in a whisper.

Emma stood back, the map all but forgotten. "It's heavy," she stated.

"Well, why don't you open it?" Gregor suggested.

JT looked at Emma with a grimace. "You know, Emma, Annabelle would want us to open it!" JT said with a smile.

"All right," Emma said quietly as she undid the tie. She peered into the bag and caught a glimpse of something gold. She reached inside and gently pulled out a large diamond ring surrounded by numerous smaller diamonds. It was obviously a wedding ring that seemed to be four carats or more. Emma held it up to the light.

"Here we go again!" JT whispered. Emma nodded and handed the ring to JT for safekeeping.

Gregor looked at the few remaining unopened pieces of furniture. "Let's keep going; you never know who saw us come in here. If there is anything else of value, I'd like to get it over to the bank!" he exclaimed.

"Good idea," JT replied. "Emma, you keep going through this desk and we will take the rest."

It wasn't long till Gregor let out a cry. He was standing up and holding a mess of bills.

Emma and JT moved quickly to his side. The deepest drawer of the chest was stacked full of bills that were obviously not United States currency. Gregor removed a stack and handed it to JT. "Not sure what country this comes from, but there sure is a lot of it!" he exclaimed.

"I think those are German Goldmarks," Emma chimed in. "I've had a few boarders try to pay with them."

Gregor grabbed one of the sheets covering the furniture. He laid the stacks of bills onto it and folded it over several times, creating a makeshift bag.

An hour later, they had discovered nothing new. They stepped outside the warehouse, locked the door, and hurried to the bank.

As they scooted up the bank steps, a rifle shot rang out. The bullet just missed JT, embedding itself in the pillar next to him. He turned, quickly sliding out his Colt and spotting the shooter on top of the livery stable. He fanned his Colt as he pushed Emma through the bank doors. Another shot took the hat off of Gregor as he dove into the bank.

Quickly closing the door, JT glanced at his friends. "Are you both okay?" he asked.

Emma and Gregor nodded. "You two stay here, I will check this out," he said, as he headed toward the back door. He stepped out gingerly, fully expecting a second shooter, but all he heard was the sound of a galloping horse.

JT quickly ran into the livery, nodded at Buck, and quickly saddled Pete. "Can I borrow those rifles I gave you?" he asked.

"You bet!" said Buck, handing him the well-worn Winchester. "Do you want the Sharps too?"

"Absolutely," JT replied, taking it and pocketing a handful of cartridges. After putting both weapons in their scabbards, JT finished saddling Pete. He mounted, yelled "Thanks!", and bolted out the door.

Chapter Three

JT soon spied a single set of fresh tracks. They were deep and wide, obviously made by a galloping horse. JT had no doubt that this was the person who shot at him.

He said to Pete, "Give me all you have and I'll give you an apple or two." Pete nodded with a snort and stretched out his long legs. JT never whipped his horse, nor did he have any spurs. He just didn't believe in them. He knew Pete would not stop until he ran himself to death.

They galloped all out for nearly ten minutes until he saw a distant cloud of dust. With a smile, JT stopped Pete and checked the Winchester and the Sharps. Both were old but well-tended and loaded for bear. He nudged Pete, and off they went like a bat out of hell. They gained quickly on the horse and rider as the dust got closer and closer. Looking down at the tracks, he could tell they were slowing down.

At 300 yards he stopped and took out the Sharps, while Pete stood dead still. JT did a quick calculation, aiming high and to the right. He pulled the trigger and the Sharps bucked. The back-shooter grabbed his right shoulder, nearly falling off his horse.

JT eased Pete forward at a slower pace. There was blood on the trail and the horseman was slumping over, holding on to his horse's mane. Soon, the man fell to the ground and his horse drifted off. JT pulled out his Winchester and rode up cautiously, keeping an eye on the six-gun the man was wearing. As he approached, the man jerked his Colt out of its holster and raised it toward JT. Before he could fire, JT put a slug in his belly. The man dropped his Colt and grabbed his bloody stomach.

JT put the Winchester back in its scabbard, removed his father's Colt, and rode up. As he dismounted and squatted next to him, he could see that the man was obviously in pain. "Who the hell are you, and why did you try to back shoot me?" JT demanded.

The man looked up. "Wanted poster in my back pocket," he whispered, then let out a soft wail and died.

JT sighed, rolled him over, and took the poster out of his pocket. He stood up and unfolded it. "Wh-what-the-hell?" he stammered. He was looking at a likeness of himself and the words "Wanted Dead. $10,000 reward." He looked at the dead man and shook his head.

JT walked to Pete and stroked his neck as he gave him a hat full of water. "Nice job, buddy," he said, as his four-legged friend pawed at the ground in acknowledgment. The dead shooter's horse was only a few yards away, looking all used up, so JT took his hat over and gave him the rest of the water. He decided to leave the dead man there for now rather than making the exhausted horse haul him back to town. He thought about ground tethering the horse but decided it was too tired to wander off very far.

JT took the dead man's Colt and Winchester, mounted Pete, and turned toward town. "We will take our time, Pete," he said to the animal. "I need to think about this wanted poster."

He pulled it out of his back pocket again to read the fine print. It said that the reward for his corpse would be paid for by Barnabas Poe, Attorney at Law in St. Louis. JT shook his head; he had never seen a wanted poster that simply said DEAD. In his experience, it was either alive or dead or alive. Someone wanted him dead badly, and he thought he knew who the culprit was.

Marcus Payne.

Chapter Four

Xavier Duvall hung another wanted poster in another chilly Colorado town as he made his way toward Gillette, a small town near Cripple Creek. Born and raised on the east coast, he had never been this far west and he didn't like it at all. Most of the people he met had a funny accent and seemed a bit too relaxed for his taste. He always had been a fast-talking, straight-ahead, take-no-prisoners kind of guy. He missed New York and his drinking buddies, but because he was a wanted man there, he knew he might never return.

As he traveled the state he marveled at the many small towns, most of which had no marshal or sheriff, which suited him just fine. He pinned his badge on selectively, taking it off when there were lawmen around and putting it on when there weren't. He had lost track of the towns he visited in the month plus since he left St. Louis but he knew he had created a stir with the posters.

Duvall was looking forward to meeting Sheriff Perez and the gang he rode with. Perez was a wanted man just like himself. He had ridden the Owl Hoot trail until he and his gang landed in Gillette. There, he greased the palm of the corrupt mayor, who appointed him sheriff. Until recently, he and his deputized gang ruled the town with an iron fist. But his initial payment to the mayor was long gone and he and his gang were wearing out their welcome. Additionally, his men had become restless, so when his old drinking buddy Marcus Payne gave him a chance to make $10,000, he jumped at it.

≈ ≈ ≈ ≈ ≈

JT rode up to Buck's, still thinking about the wanted poster. "Well, did you catch him?" Buck inquired.

"I surely did," JT said with a smile as he dismounted.

Buck took Pete's reins. "Well, where is he?"

"He is down the trail with a horse that he damn near rode to death," JT said. "I would have brought him back but his horse was just too darned exhausted. I'd appreciate it if you would take your buckboard out there and retrieve both of them."

Buck glanced over at him. "Well, I could do that. But is he going to shoot at me like he did with you?"

JT laughed. "I don't think so. He is dancing with the devil as we speak. But if you could do it before dark you can have his horse."

"Okay, will do," Buck chuckled. "But I may have to build another stable with all the darn horses you're bringing me."

"Not a bad problem, is it? Anyway, take the dead man over to the deputies to see if he is wanted. No sense letting a bounty go to waste." JT paused, looking at a sturdy mule in the back of the livery. "Where did you get that mule?"

"Oh, that's from a widowed farmer. Her husband just up and died, and she is moving back to Pennsylvania. She gave me quite the deal on him."

"He's a fine-looking mule. I'd like to buy him from you if he's for sale."

Buck half laughed and half snorted. "Are you kidding me? He's all yours, after all the horses, rifles, and gold you've given me!"

"Well thank you kindly. I accept."

"Now you're talking. And the widow threw in some great big saddlebags—take them as well!"

They shook on the deal, and JT headed for the boarding house.

≈ ≈ ≈ ≈ ≈

He was greeted on the porch by Gregor and Emma. Dr. DeWitt soon appeared with his helper and sweetheart Dawn on his arm. She sprang forward to give JT a hug. "Oh, we've missed you so much!" she exclaimed.

DeWitt clasped JT's shoulder and gripped his hand. "It's good to have you back, sir," he said solemnly. "I deeply regret your—indeed, all of our—loss."

JT smiled. "It's good to see you all again. I need to show you something, but I'd like to get cleaned up first. How about an early supper at the hotel café at five?"

Everyone agreed, and Gregor spoke up. "That would be fine. By the way, we put the new finds in the safe at the bank."

JT looked up. "Lord, I'd almost forgotten about that. That's great, I appreciate it. Okay, I'll see you all at supper."

He headed up the stairs to his suite. Inside, he pulled out the poster from his back pocket and spread it out on the bed. His likeness was spot on and the words "WANTED, DEAD" jumped out at him. He saw that his body needed to be turned in to a lawyer by the name of Barnabas Poe in St. Louis to claim the $10,000.

"GOD DAMN YOU, MARCUS PAYNE!" he shouted.

Chapter Five

Jean Cantrell was enjoying herself. She had cut and dyed her hair, put on a dress, and was dealing faro in an upscale saloon in Yuma, Colorado. The owner had wanted her to return to her old ways and entertain the cowboys in her bed, but she talked him into letting her deal instead. She was cheating and the owner knew it, but since she was doubling what his former dealer took in, she was well worth the 15% cut of the take he paid her.

Jean's last bank job in the town of Point Stevens Pass had not gone well, and she was mourning the loss of her brother Cain. JT Thomas had gunned him down in a bar back in her former home of Lakeview.

Jean had raised Cain after their parents died of cholera. They had always been a good team, like peas in a pod. Cain loved money, women, and good whiskey, but what he really loved was robbing banks. He said it made him feel in control of his life. Jean agreed, and because he let her call the shots it usually worked out well. She missed him dearly since he really had been her only friend, and she planned on avenging his death one way or another.

It was early and the saloon was nearly empty. Jean finished dealing to the lone man sitting at the faro table. The scruffy hombre lost again and stood up from the table.

"Damn little lady, I'm not sure how you are doing it, but you sure are lucky. You cleaned me out," he said, showing his empty wallet.

Jean smiled. "Well, come back when you're rich again and we will have another go!"

The man pulled out a wanted poster from his back pocket and laid it on the table. "Oh, you bet I will. I'll be back with $10,000, and maybe you and I can get really acquainted. And I ain't talking about playing faro!" he exclaimed.

Jean laughed. "Well, for $10,000 I might oblige you," she said with a smirk as she looked down at the poster. Her mouth fell open as she stared at a drawing of JT Thomas. The man reached for the poster but Jean put her hand on it. "Where did you get this?" she asked.

"Over at the empty jail. It was pinned right next to the door," the man replied.

Jean reached into her dress pocket, pulled out two silver dollars, and handed them to the man. "I'll keep the poster if you don't mind," she said with a frown.

The man looked down at the coins and nodded. "Thanks. I know where to find more," he said, as he headed toward the bar.

Jean stood up and put a small sign that said "CLOSED" on the table. She went upstairs to her room and packed up her meager belongings, then slipped out and walked down the stairs, stopping at the bar. She slid her room key to the bartender. "I'm quitting," she said with a grin. "I've got $10,000 to make and an old score to settle!"

≈ ≈ ≈ ≈ ≈

JT arrived early at the hotel café. He pointed to a large table along the back wall with a view of the front door. "I'd like that table," he said to the maître d' and slipped him a five-dollar gold piece. "My pleasure, sir," the man said and led him to the table.

JT sat down with his back against the wall, his Winchester next to him, and his father's Colt on the table. Dawn and DeWitt arrived shortly afterward. Dawn gave the seated JT an awkward hug and kiss. A few minutes later, Emma and Gregor strode up to the table. JT did not rise, keeping an eye on the door.

"Please sit down and make yourselves comfortable," JT said, as he pulled the wanted poster out of his pocket. He passed it first to Gregor, who immediately recognized what it was. Gregor passed it to Emma while looking at JT.

"Damn him," Gregor snarled.

"What, what?" Dawn asked, as Emma passed the poster to her. The blood drained out of her face as she passed it to the doctor. "What is this about?" she asked, looking around the table. "I don't understand. Why in the world would you be wanted, JT?"

The doctor whispered in her ear and her eyes got as large as saucers. "That can't be," she said. "Who would do such a thing?"

Simultaneously, JT and Gregor uttered "Marcus Payne."

The waiter, who had been standing discreetly away from the table, tentatively approached. JT looked up, beckoning him to come closer. "Would you like to start with a beverage?" the waiter asked formally.

JT laughed out loud. "Oh yes, absolutely, absolutely. Make mine Scotch—a double!"

After the waiter took drink orders, JT looked at his friends. "I know Gregor has told you about what happened in New York, but I surely never expected this. This has to be the work of Marcus Payne."

Dawn spoke up. "But he is in prison! How could he do this?"

Gregor chuckled. "Oh, he has plenty of money, and I'm guessing Sheriff Xavier Duvall is leading the charge on this."

JT nodded. "Without a doubt."

Emma leaned toward JT. "So, what are we going to do about this? We certainly can't let it stand!" she exclaimed.

"Certainly not," DeWitt said, as he slammed down his fist down the table.

After the waiter returned with their drinks, JT looked around the table. "I may have a plan, but I would like all of you to give me your own ideas as well," he said, picking up his glass and taking a hefty drink.

≈ ≈ ≈ ≈ ≈

Sheriff Duvall rode up to the Red Eye Saloon in Gillette. Pushing his way through the swinging doors, he made his way to the bar, nodded at the bartender, and placed a twenty-dollar gold coin on the bar. "Beer and your best whiskey," he ordered. "Tell me, do you know where I can find Sheriff Perez?"

"Well, he is probably over at the jail, but his deputies are over in the corner drinking rotgut and playing poker with peanut shells," the bartender said with a derisive snort. "Hey Bart! This man is looking for the sheriff!" he shouted.

Bart Wiggins, one of Perez's right-hand men, looked over at the sheriff's badge pinned on Duvall. "Are you Sheriff Duvall?" he asked, with the gravelly voice of a smoker.

Duvall picked up his beer and proceeded to drain it, nodding at the bartender to get him another. "That would be me," he replied. "Why don't you go get the sheriff and I'll buy you and your friends a drink. Perez too, if he is a drinking man."

Bart jumped up. "Oh, he is, he is. I'll go and fetch him. He's been expecting you," he said, and blew through the batwing doors.

Duvall turned to the bartender. "Two bottles of what I'm drinking, over there," he said. He walked over to the table and took the seat vacated by Bart Wiggins, placing his saddlebags next to him on the floor.

"You boys are deputies, right?" he asked with a smile.

"Yes, we are," the man seated next to him replied.

"Well, your days of playing for peanut shells are long gone," he said, handing each of the men a ten-dollar gold piece. The deputies smiled as the bartender set the bottles in the middle of the table. Their grins grew even larger as each man dumped his rotgut on the floor and filled a glass with the good stuff.

Bart Wiggins pushed through the doors, followed by Sheriff Perez. One of the deputies grabbed two chairs from the next table as Duvall stood up to shake Perez's hand.

"Mighty glad to meet you, Duvall," Perez said. "What took you so long? We've been expecting you for weeks."

"Well, I was in no hurry and stopped at quite a few towns on the way. Never been to Colorado before," Duvall replied. "By the way, Marcus Payne said to say hello, and he appreciates you helping him out."

Perez smirked. "For $10,000, I'm glad to help anybody. Anyway, nice to meet you too, and sorry to hear Marcus is in prison. Sit down and tell me all about it."

The bartender brought two more glasses and Duvall looked around the table. "You got my wires and the letter Marcus sent you, right? What did you share with these men?"

"Just that if we kill a man named JT Thomas, we will all be rich!"

Duvall laughed. "That pretty much sums it up, but you are going to have competition," he said, as spread out the wanted poster.

Perez looked up. "What the hell is this?"

Duvall reached into his saddlebag and pulled out a hefty bag filled with gold coins. "Marcus said you probably needed an incentive, so I've been putting up a few wanted posters on my own for a while. But here is the deal," he said, "this gold is your up-front money. It's damn near $3,000 and the $10,000 is on top of that!"

Perez smiled as he grabbed the bag. "Well, now we are talking. Let's get this show on the road!"

Chapter Six

JT met his friends at his usual table in the back of the hotel café. When everyone was seated, Gregor Nelson spoke up.

"I think we need to meet this head on. You are a man of wealth and can hire the best attorneys. I'm sure St. Louis has some excellent firms," he said.

"I agree," DeWitt chimed in, "but that means someone needs to go to St. Louis, and it shouldn't be JT. He needs to lay low for a while until we get this sorted out." Everyone nodded.

Emma turned to Gregor. "It seems this St. Louis lawyer Barnabas Poe is behind these wanted posters. How about if you had your pals at the Pinkerton agency put a little fear into him? From what I'm told they are pretty good at that!" she exclaimed.

Gregor laughed. "Well, it depends on who you choose, but I do know a few who'd be happy to scare the hell out of him. A couple of them would shoot him on sight if JT paid them enough!"

JT chuckled. "Let's hold off on shooting him for now, but I think your ideas make a lot of sense. With those posters out on me, I surely don't want to be walking around in St. Louis, or anywhere else for that matter. And yes, I certainly can afford it. Gregor, I think you should be the one to go to St. Louis, on my nickel of course."

Gregor nodded. "I'd be glad to. Perhaps your lawyers in New York could give us a referral."

JT leaned forward. "That's an excellent idea. In fact, let's hire them to collaborate on this thing as well. We may need their help with Marcus Payne in New York. If he isn't stopped, he will just keep doing this."

Gregor thumped the table. "Good! I will leave the day after tomorrow."

Emma looked over at JT. "I think perhaps you should get back to your cabin until this gets resolved," she said.

JT shook his head. "Well, yes and no. I didn't share this with you, but three scruffy hombres actually found my cabin and knew about the $10,000 reward. I don't know how they found it because it's well off the beaten path."

DeWitt frowned and hung his head. "I'm sorry, that was my fault. I was having a drink in the saloon and three men were asking about you. They said they were friends of yours, so I told them how to find your place."

"They didn't waste any time," JT said. "They were sitting at my table when I got there. But I dealt with them—sent them to hell." JT paused and smiled. "Anyway, there are three less bounty hunters to worry about, and Buck's assistant now has a new horse and saddle!"

DeWitt ruefully shook his head. "I'm sorry, JT. I confess my judgment was clouded a bit by too much whiskey."

"Well, that's water under the bridge, and now I know I can at least use the cabin without being found. But I'm not really one to run and hide and I can't sit still for long. I'll give Gregor some time to get things started, then check back here in a week."

"Make it ten days and I'll meet you here or at your cabin, whichever you would prefer," Gregor replied.

"Let's make it here," JT replied. "I'll probably need to resupply by then as well. Meanwhile, I'll try to keep busy by working on the cabin and cooking. There are a few recipes I learned in New York I'd like to try."

Emma looked surprised. "I didn't know you could cook," she said.

JT smiled. "Oh, I'm just an amateur cook, but I enjoy it. And as my old man used to say, "If you don't eat you die.""

Chapter Seven

Jean Cantrell slowly made her way toward Point Stevens Pass. She thought about going into town in her new disguise, but decided instead to camp on the outskirts to think things over. She had no idea if JT Thomas was in town, but it was a place to start. If caught, she knew she would hang. On the other hand, $10,000 was a lot of money. Besides, JT had killed her brother Cain and she needed to settle the score. She had no idea who was still in town, but she hoped Emily and Dawn were killed in the fire Cain had started. "Boy, I wish I had seen that. I do love a good blaze!" she murmured to herself.

But right now, what she needed was a plan. Looking at the stream next to her campsite, she remembered that fishing helped her think. She cut a pole, found a few earthworms under rocks, and took her fishing gear out of her saddlebags.

She sat on the bank of the stream, thinking about her next step. There were a couple of small saloons in town. One was known for its "soiled doves." Maybe with her new disguise, she could sneak into town at midnight and apply for a job. She hated to return to whoring, but she knew the best way to get information was in bed with drunken cowboys. And hell, she could use the money. She could stay in her room during the day and get all the gossip and information she needed without ever leaving the saloon.

Just then, she felt a tug on her line and yanked a nice-sized trout out of the water. She smiled as she spoke to her horse. "See? Fishing really *is* good for thinking. And I do love trout!"

≈≈≈≈≈

Gregor arrived in St. Louis, having previously sent a wire to his employer Attorney Mort Bernstein in New York. Bernstein quickly replied with a referral for a senior attorney named Drew Morrow in St. Louis. He made his way to the attorney's office, intending to schedule an appointment. Instead, he was ushered to a conference room by the law firm's receptionist and was surprised to see Attorney Morrow already seated. Drew stood up to shake Gregor's hand and nodded for him to sit. Gregor guessed that Morrow was in his mid-forties. He was tall and thin, with a full head of dark brown hair and a friendly manner about him.

"Would you like a cup of coffee?" the attorney asked.

"No, but thank you," Gregor replied. "You come highly recommended by my employer Morton Bernstein."

"Yes, Mort cabled me and told me to expect you today," Morrow replied. "How is he?"

"Last time I saw him he was as fit as a fiddle," said Gregor. He then launched into a full explanation of why he was there, and finished by spreading JT's wanted poster on the table.

Morrow stood up and poured himself a cup of coffee. He gazed out the window for a moment, then sat back down. "That is quite an interesting story. Now I know why Mort sent you to our firm. We have a history with Barnabas Poe, and your characterization of him is spot on. He is slimy and unscrupulous. He has nearly been disbarred more than once, but he's been too slippery to charge. But if we can prove his part in this, I would think that will be the straw that breaks Poe's back and finally gets him out of our profession."

Gregor sat up straight. "That is indeed good news. Tell me, what would you suggest?"

Morrow stared at the ceiling for what seemed like an eternity. Finally, he sat up straight and looked Gregor in the eye. "I believe our immediate course of action should be to write a letter to the Bar Association and petition the court to get Barnabas Poe to cease and desist. After that, we should have our own poster made up, rescinding the bounty. Your suggestion of hiring Pinkerton is a good one. And as this firm happens to have the ear of the governor, perhaps Mr. Thomas might make a generous contribution to his reelection campaign. His support could be crucial."

"An excellent plan," Gregor replied. "JT has authorized me to do and spend whatever is necessary!"

"Good. Perhaps we should coordinate with Mort Bernstein to freeze Marcus Payne's assets in New York."

"Well, great minds think alike. That is exactly what Bernstein said. He also mentioned revenge, served cold," Gregor said with a chuckle.

Morrow grinned. "That sounds like the Mort Bernstein we both know and love!"

Chapter Eight

Duvall and Perez led their men toward Point Stevens Pass under a chilly late October sky. One of Perez's deputies had a sister there who had told him about Emma's boarding house fire and JT's pursuit of the Cantrells, so Duvall thought it sounded like a good place to start. The red-eyed deputies had made their way through numerous bottles of whiskey, playing poker into the wee hours. Some were slumped in their saddles, and Perez had to remind them to fill their canteens.

The trip was fairly uneventful and longer than Duvall thought it would be, but he used the time to get to know Perez and each of the deputies. He learned that all but one of them were wanted men who had ridden the Owl Hoot Trail, robbing and marauding travelers until they established themselves as "the law" in Gillette. Being a wanted man himself, he thought it was a pretty good arrangement.

The gang pulled up a mile outside of Point Stevens Pass, making camp and sorting through their options. Duvall and Perez pulled out a bottle of rye and sat down on a log as they watched the men go about their camp duties. "I'm thinking that you shouldn't go into town. If JT is there, he will recognize you," Perez said.

Duvall nodded. "Yeah, that wouldn't be a good idea."

"Let's send in Tim Yates to meet with his sister. He's the only one of us the law's not looking for."

Duvall nodded. "Well, that's handy."

"Hey Yates, come on over here," Perez yelled across the camp.

Yates hustled over and Perez handed him the bottle of rye. Pulling the cork, he said, "Yeah boss, what's up?"

"Well, we were thinking you could go into town by yourself and talk to your sister, maybe get the lay of the land," Perez replied.

Yates took a pull on the whiskey. "Sure, I can do that," he said, looking at the sky. "You want me to leave now or in the morning?"

Duvall spoke up. "Best to go now. Stay overnight and take a pack horse or two with you so you can stock up in the morning."

Yates nodded and took another long swig from the bottle. "I'll do that," he replied.

Duvall pulled JT's wanted poster and a wad of bills out of his pocket and handed them over. "Okay, then get going." He took the bottle back. "And take it easy on the booze while you're there. You can drink as much as you like once we kill JT Thomas!"

JT woke up early and made his way to the livery. A sleepy Buck was placing the last of the supplies JT had picked up the night before on the new mule, having already saddled up Pete and having loaded up Re-Pete. "Looks like you're gonna be cooking up a storm," he said, yawning.

JT smiled and nodded. "Well, with any luck I won't have much else to do. I'll be back in ten days or so." He headed out of the livery after carefully surveying the rooftops for a shooter, then led his small caravan toward the trail.

He took his time getting to his cabin, taking a different route than his normal one. He wasn't so sure that he was safe at the cabin since there was no telling how many people had overheard the directions the tipsy doctor had given to the bounty hunters. Also, bartenders hear darn near everything that is said at the bar. He really didn't know the bartender, but with $10, 000 on his head he was not about to trust anyone.

He stopped often to check his back trail and enjoyed the new route to the cabin. The mountain views were spectacular, and the sun shone through a cloudless sky. JT didn't even mind the chill in the air. He had spent a lot of time in Wisconsin and welcomed the change of seasons.

On the other hand, he knew his new fur-lined winter coat, hat and gloves were going to come in handy. "Boy, it sure is nice to be wealthy!" he said to himself.

≈ ≈ ≈ ≈ ≈

Jean Cantrell made her way down the stairs of Buffalo Bob's saloon as the sun was setting in a cloudless, chilly sky. She had made a deal with Bob, or Buffalo, as he preferred to be called. She was back to whoring again, but she had negotiated three meals a day in the saloon and never needed to leave the premises. She told Buffalo that she was hiding from her husband and needed to lay low for a while. Bob, never looking up from Jean's cleavage, readily agreed as long as he got a free sample every day in her bed.

Buffalo was chatting with a man at the near-empty bar while cleaning a beer glass. As Jean began to make her way into the kitchen for her supper, he looked up. "Hey Jean, come meet my brother," he said.

Jean spun on her heels, put on a smile, and sauntered over to the bar with her hand outstretched. The brother reached out, bent at the waist, and kissed the top of her hand. "I am so glad to finally meet you!" he said.

Jean looked over at Buffalo quizzically as he laughed. "He has been wanting to meet you since I told him about you. His name is Adrian and he is the bartender at the Stevens Saloon."

Jean smiled at Adrian. Pleased to meet you," she said.

The pleasure is all mine," replied Adrian.

"Adrian works the same hours as I do, so he really can't get over here when you are working. I thought if he came early you might put off supper and accommodate him," Buffalo said.

Adrian took out a five-dollar gold coin and set it on the bar. "I'll pay double your going rate," he said.

Jean laughed. "Well, Mr. Hand-kissing Adrian, double will be just dandy. Give me a minute to freshen up and come on up. Bring some of that good Scotch Buffalo keeps in the back room and we will get well acquainted."

Adrian and Buffalo smiled and nodded as Jean slowly made her way up the stairs, knowing both horny men were watching her. "We don't kiss hands in my room, but maybe I'll kiss something else for you," she said over her shoulder.

Chapter Nine

On his second day in St. Louis, Gregor Nelson walked into the office of Tillson, Morrow, and Campbell. He was ushered into Drew Morrow's office by his assistant. "Coffee, Mr. Nelson?" the man asked.

"No thanks. I've been up since the crack of dawn and am all coffeed out," he replied.

Morrow arrived and waved him into a seat in front of his desk. The office was spacious and neat as a pin, and Gregor nodded to himself approvingly.

Morrow smiled. "Well, I have good news for you so don't get too comfortable. We have an audience with the governor in an hour from now. I hope you brought a few of those gold coins you offered me yesterday!"

Gregor laughed. "Absolutely, and that is indeed good news."

The attorney handed Gregor a draft of his letter to the Bar Association. "Read this. If you approve, we will send it post-haste."

Gregor carefully looked over the letter and handed it back. "Looks fine to me, but you are the expert," he said.

Morrow nodded and handed over the cease and desist letter addressed to Barnabas Poe.

Gregor held up his hands. "I don't need to read that. Just do what you need to do!" he exclaimed.

Morrow laughed and nodded as he stood up. "Well then, let's get over to the governor's mansion. We don't want to be late—he hates tardiness!"

≈ ≈ ≈ ≈ ≈

Gregor and Morrow dismounted from the carriage and made their way up the governor's mansion steps, where a federal marshal stood guarding the huge double doors.

"Good morning Mr. Morrow," the marshal said with a smile.

Morrow stuck out his hand. "Well, James Benson. How are you?"

"I'm very good, thank you for asking. I haven't seen you since our court encounter," the man replied.

Morrow laughed and turned to Gregor. "James and I had a bit of a dust-up in court recently!" he said.

"A dust-up? More like I was dirt and you were cleaning up!"

"Hey, my client was innocent and I just needed to make sure the jury understood that," Morrow stated with a grin.

"Oh, indeed they did. My hat's off to you; you certainly earned your money. But let's get going. You know how the governor is about being late."

Benson led the way into the mansion. Inside the outer office, he nodded to the assistant and knocked on the governor's door.

"Come in, come in!" a booming voice resonated from within.

Benson opened the door and waved Gregor and Morrow inside. The governor stood up from his desk, looking at the watch in his hand. "Right on time, nicely done, nicely done," he said, as he came around the desk and shook hands with his visitors.

Morrow put his hand on Gregor's shoulder. "Governor Fletcher, I'd like to introduce you to Mr. Gregor Nelson. He has an interesting story that you need to hear. He also wants to discuss your reelection campaign fund!"

Fletcher smiled widely and grabbed Gregor's hand with a firm grip, pumping it up and down. "Wonderful, wonderful. Please sit down," he said, pointing to the leather chairs in front of his desk. Looking at the marshal, he said, "James, perhaps you should stay. We don't want any accusations of shenanigans about a donation, do we?"

Benson smiled and motioned for Morrow and Gregor to sit down as he leaned against the door jamb.

Governor Fletcher looked at Morrow. "How have you been, Drew? I haven't seen you since, gosh, the Christmas ball!"

"It has been a long time. I am busy, but well!" Morrow replied.

"Well, from what the marshal tells me you have been knocking them dead in the courtroom. Perhaps we could talk you into coming over to our side as a prosecutor!"

Morrow laughed. "I don't think so. I know what you pay them!"

"Yes, I know, the almighty dollar. But it's good to see you, and I'm glad you are doing well. By the way, I had lunch with your father last week. He certainly is enjoying his retirement! I still say your father was the best prosecutor I have ever met. We surely miss him. Anyway, I'm on a tight schedule, so what can I do for you?"

Morrow leaned forward. "It's quite an interesting story. I'll let Mr. Nelson tell it and fill in when necessary."

Gregor sat up and got to the point quickly. "I am representing a Mr. JT Thomas, who is currently living in Colorado. This story actually starts with four women being rescued by JT..."

Gregor quickly told the tale from beginning to end, with a detailed account of JT's murder trial and the subsequent conviction of Marcus Payne. He ended with the role of fugitive Sheriff Xavier Duvall and the wanted posters that called for JT's death.

Morrow chimed in. "Barnabas Poe is well known to us at Tillson, Morrow, and Campbell. We have had run-ins with him before, and all I can say is he needs to be either tarred and feathered and run out of town or disbarred. Preferably both!"

The marshal chuckled, and Fletcher looked at him. "You are laughing, James. Do you know this Barnabas Poe?"

"Oh yes, indeed," Benson replied. "He is a crook in sheep's clothing. I for one would be happy to coat the man in tar then shoot the son of a bitch!"

"Oh, my," the governor said, looking across the desk at Gregor and Drew. "If my trusted marshal has such a low opinion of this man, then, by all means, he needs to be stopped immediately!"

"Perhaps we should simply arrest Mr. Poe?" Benson suggested.

Fletcher frowned. "Can we do that? What would be the charge?"

"Oh, I'm sure we can come up with a charge. With everything he's done, we could probably just spook him into resisting arrest!"

Morrow laughed out loud. "I love it!"

"Today is Thursday. How about if I have one of my men watch Mr. Poe throughout the day tomorrow, then we arrest him after the courts close on Friday? That way, good old Barnabas Poe can spend the weekend in jail with the roughest cellmates we can find. We can drop the charges on Monday, but by God we will have to put a scare into him!" Benson exclaimed.

"And how about I have my Pinkerton friends shadow him after he gets out and continue the scare tactics?" Gregor asked, grinning.

Fletcher smiled. "An excellent plan." He checked his pocket watch. "Now get out of here and get to it. I'm late for my next meeting and I hate being late!"

He stood up and shook Gregor's hand with an expectant look on his face. Gregor grinned and reached into his coat, pulled out a roll of cash, and pressed it into the governor's hand. "Here is $2,000 for your campaign. I'm only sorry I can't vote for you!"

Fletcher smiled as he handed the wad of bills to the marshal. "This will do just fine, and it is most appreciated!"

Chapter Ten

Tim Yates rode up to his sister's house in Point Stevens Pass. His alcohol buzz was subsiding, but he figured she'd have whiskey inside. He opened the gate on the white picket fence that enclosed the front yard, noticing the flowers and the well-kept property. Yates smiled to himself, thinking *That's my sister, everything in its proper place. And she always loved flowers.* He knocked on the door, waited, and knocked again.

"I'm coming, I'm coming. Hold your horses!" a feminine voice sounded out through the door.

The door opened. His sister stood there with an apron on and a ladle in her hand. "My God, Timmy!" she screamed as she stepped forward to give him a bear hug.

"Hello, Sarah," he said, grinning.

"Look who is here," she yelled, as her husband Philip appeared with a baby in his arms.

"Hello Tim, welcome! It's good to see you!" Philip said.

Sarah motioned him toward the kitchen. "You are just in time for dinner. Come and sit at the table; I need a few more minutes. Would you like a drink?"

Tim smiled. "Oh, only if you are having one!"

Sarah laughed. "Oh, you are so sweet, Timmy. If this isn't a special occasion, I don't know what is!"

She called over her shoulder as she headed for the kitchen. "Phil, could you put the baby back in his crib? Pour Timmy some whiskey, and I'll have a glass of wine," she said, with joy in her voice.

After dinner, Sarah excused herself to check on the baby while Phil cleaned up the kitchen. Tim offered to help and was assigned to dry the dishes. When they finished, Phil poured another glass of wine for Sarah, then reached over to top off Tim's whiskey.

"You're not drinking, Phil?" Tim inquired.

"No, I haven't had a drink in over a year. When I found out Sarah was pregnant, I gave it up. I'd like to grow old and healthy for my son, and for your lovely sister as well"! he stated quietly. Sarah smiled and patted his hand.

"Well, good for you. I'm proud of you," Tim said.

Phil grinned. "So, what brings you back to Point Stevens Pass?" he inquired.

Tim pulled out the wanted poster and spread it on the kitchen table. "I'm looking for this guy," he said.

"Why in the world would you do that?" Sarah exclaimed.

"Well, he is wanted," Tim said quietly, "and $10,000 is a lot of money."

"Oh, pshaw," Sarah said with a frown. "You don't need blood money. Why don't you come work for Phil in the tonsorial parlor? Phil could teach you to cut hair and you would make an honest living!"

"Well that's a mighty nice offer, but you know me. I really need to work out in the open air, not behind four walls. Now tell me, have you seen this man recently?"

Phil frowned and spoke up. "Yes, I gave him a haircut about a week ago. He was staying at the hotel, but I haven't seen him lately."

Sarah said, "Tim, we have met JT and he is a really nice guy. People call him 'the good egg,' and he really is. This wanted poster is probably not even legal."

Phil leaned forward, sipping his coffee. "She is right, Tim, and besides, he is not someone to go up against. He was a federal marshal who cleaned up a wild town in Kansas. Word is, he is deadly with both a Winchester and a Sharps. Half the people he's gunned down never saw it coming, and he's just as good with a pistol."

Sarah grimaced. "Tim, he is right. Give this up."

Tim looked at his sister. "Well, I'll think about it, but I've got some friends counting on me. Anyhow, do you think I could stay in your guest room tonight? I'd be gone in the morning."

Phil responded quickly. "I'm sorry, Tim. The guest room is now the baby's room, and you really don't want to be in there. He can be real fussy at night."

Sarah nodded at Tim. "How about if we buy you a night at the hotel? It is very nice. Also, JT Thomas eats there sometimes. If you meet him and get to know him, I'm sure you'll give up on this crazy idea."

Tim stood up. "God bless you sis, but I don't need your money. In fact, why don't you buy a little something for the baby" he said, placing a twenty-dollar bill on the table. "I will check into the hotel, then I'll stop by in the morning to say goodbye." He picked up his hat and headed for the door, nodding to Phil. "Maybe I'll stop in for a haircut before I leave. It's been a while!"

$$\approx \approx \approx \approx \approx$$

Tim dropped his horse off at Buck's livery. He was walking toward the hotel at the other end of the main street when he saw the Stevens Saloon. He paused. *Oh, why not? The night is young and maybe I can get a room there too.*

He walked into the saloon and up to the bar. "Hello, Tim Yates!" the bartender called out. "Long time no see!"

Tim grinned at the bartender. "Hey Adrian! How you been?"

"I can't complain. What can I get you? First drink is on the house!"

"Well then, how about a shot of Kentucky bourbon? And leave the bottle," Yates said, as he took out the wad of bills and slapped them on the bar.

Adrian looked at the cash and grinned. "A bottle of my best Kenn-tu-kee Wis-KEE coming up!"

Tim looked around the bar. He noticed Doctor DeWitt sitting at a table, playing cards and drinking rye. He nodded at a few cowboys he knew, who smiled and waved back.

Adrian returned with the bottle and two glasses, pouring both of them to the brim and sliding one over to Tim. Picking up the other, he clicked it on Tim's glass. "Welcome back. Looks like you're doing pretty well for yourself, Mr. Yates."

"Well, I've got some friends that are doing okay," Tim said, as he spread JT's wanted poster on the bar. "Have you seen this guy?"

Adrian looked at the poster and frowned. "Well, yeah, but what the hell are you doing? Tim, this guy will eat you up and spit you out."

Tim smiled. "Well, I'll have help, and he doesn't look so tough."

Adrian looked at the poster again. "Well, it's your funeral, Timmy boy, but don't say I didn't warn you. And yes, I saw him last week, standing right where you are. I think he was staying over at the hotel. But I haven't seen him for a while, though he usually comes in here quite often."

"Where else would he be?"

Adrian knew Tim to be one of the nicest guys he had ever met. He'd heard Dr. DeWitt tell the three scruffy hombres about JT's cabin, and had heard how that turned out. All three dead by JT's hand in an instant. He shook his head and said, "If he is not at the hotel, I have no idea where he could be."

Tim nodded. "Okay, thanks. Say, do you still have rooms upstairs for rent?"

The bartender nodded, glad to be off the JT Thomas subject. "You bet. For you, no charge. Why don't you take that bottle upstairs and get a good night's sleep? If you sleep on it, hopefully you'll give up on the idea. Hey, I know George McClain is hiring out on his ranch. You could spend the winter doing mighty little for twenty dollars a month and three squares a day."

Tim smiled as he grabbed his bottle. "Thanks, Adrian, you are a good friend. I'll keep that in mind."

He sauntered up the stairs, wishing the Stevens Saloon had whores. But they didn't, so he supposed he would make do with the whiskey. In any case, it was good to be back among friends and family, even if they didn't like his plan. He got to his room, collapsed on the bed, and pondered the situation.

What if they're right about this guy? Maybe I should think again on this JT Thomas deal.

Chapter Eleven

Jean had spent an interesting session with Buffalo's brother Adrian, giving him her best effort. When he lit up a hand-rolled cigarette afterward, he sighed and blew the smoke at the ceiling. Adrian had consumed more than his share of Scotch and was feeling the effects.

Jean snuggled into his chest. "That was fantastic. You really know how to make a woman feel good!" she exclaimed.

Adrian grinned. "Well, thank you darlin'. You're not so bad yourself. I'm gonna need to come back here real soon."

"That would be wonderful," Jean replied. "Say, can I ask you a question? Do you know a man called JT Thomas?"

Adrian laughed. "Yeah, I do. Don't tell me—you saw the wanted poster and want to cash in."

Jean smiled wickedly. "Well, maybe. You have to turn a lot of tricks to make $10,000!"

"Yes, I would suppose so. But no offense; you're no match for JT. And those wanted posters are bogus. JT is a rich man, and from what the doctor tells me, he is squashing the St. Louis attorney that is supposed to pay the reward."

"Well that's interesting, but believe it or not I have an old score to settle with him. Tell me where I can find him and there won't be a charge for this session."

"Well, that's mighty nice of you. Here is what I know. He had been staying at the hotel until a few days ago, but I'm told he is headed back to his cabin. If he's not there, he might be at his cave. I hear he discovered diamonds and such there, and it may even be seamed with gold."

Jean smiled. "Really? So, you're telling me he is rich?"

"Oh yes, mighty rich."

"Well, Adrian, if you give me directions to this cabin, I'll give you another go for free."

Adrian smiled. "You have a deal!"

$$\approx \approx \approx \approx \approx$$

JT surveyed his cabin and its surroundings with his spyglass. Seeing no signs of life, he rode up and unpacked the horses and mule. The cabin seemed to be just as he had left it, and he smiled as he put away the spices and dry goods he had brought along. He was looking forward to trying a new venison recipe, and he knew where to find the meat.

He picked up his Winchester and headed toward the spot where he'd seen a young buck grazing, pulling his new coat tighter. It was at least ten degrees colder here than in town, and it looked like it would be snowing by nightfall.

JT move silently through the woods, enjoying the view. He thought of Annabelle. *My God, she would have loved this.*

He crossed the creek by stepping on stones, careful not to step in the chilly water. Halfway across, he looked up and was face to face with the largest cougar he had ever seen. She was staring intently at him, close enough that he could hear her purring. He stopped in the middle of the stream and started to bring his Winchester to bear. The purring stopped abruptly, and she turned and dashed off into the forest.

JT frowned as he made his way to the bank. The cat was not only big, but had a beautiful coat of red fur, the color of Annabelle's hair. He thought he had heard the sound of a sleigh bell as the animal dashed into the woods. He shook his head. *Oh, stop. She is gone and is not coming back.*

He followed the stream to the spot where he had seen the buck. There were numerous deer tracks, some small and some large. He emptied a small sack of dried corn on the ground and headed back to the cabin. Tomorrow was another day, and he was a patient man.

Chapter Twelve

After getting a haircut from his brother-in-law and stocking up at the mercantile, Tim Yates rode into Duvall and Pérez's camp at mid-morning. The two men hurried up to him. "Well, what did you find out?" Duvall demanded.

"He is there, or at least he was. He was staying at the hotel, but the bartender said he hasn't seen him for a few days," Tim replied.

"All right! Excellent!" Duvall exclaimed.

Pérez nodded. "Let's go in tomorrow before dawn and surround the place."

The next morning, masked deputies surrounded the hotel in Point Stevens Pass. Pérez and Duvall dismounted and strode up the stairs. The clerk was dozing in a chair, feet on the counter. Pérez slapped his feet and they hit the floor with a thud. Duvall laughed out loud as the man sat up straight in the chair. "What, what!" he exclaimed.

Pérez pointed his Colt. "Is JT Thomas still registered here?"

"Ah no, no he is not. He left about a week ago," the clerk said, wide-eyed.

"You wouldn't be shittin' us? We were told he was here."

"Ah no. Like I said, he checked out!"

Duvall looked at Pérez. "Let's make sure," he said, as he pulled his Colt. "Let's round up all the guests and see if you're lying."

The clerk stood up. "You can't do that. I won't allow it!"

It was Pérez's turn to laugh. "Well, I can shoot you now and knock on the doors myself, or you can do it and I may not shoot you at all! Your choice, big guy. You have five seconds to make up your mind! One, two, three…"

"Okay, okay, I'll do it!" the man replied with a shudder.

Duvall followed the clerk up the stairs while Pérez waited below. Emma and seven guests were awakened and told to move down to the lobby. Pérez then moved them out onto the front porch and lined them up in a neat row. The masked deputies raised their rifles, each picking out a target.

Duvall and Pérez mounted up. "Well fella, I guess you were right. No JT Thomas here!" Duvall said.

"I told you so!" the clerk yelled.

"Whoa, keep it down big guy, you don't want to wake up the sheriff!" Pérez said. He looked at the sleepy guests. "So, does anyone here know JT Thomas?"

No one spoke up. "Damn, he was staying here in the hotel. I know that some of you noticed him!" Duvall said.

Emma raised her hand. "I know him, and he isn't here."

"Well no shit, we can see that. Do you know where he is?"

Emma stared straight into Duvall's eyes. "No, I don't, and I wouldn't tell you if I did. He is a friend of mine, and next time I see him I'm going to tell him what happened here. All of you will be sorry!"

Duvall raised his Colt and thumbed back the hammer. "I don't think you will do that, 'cause I'm going to kill you right now!"

Pérez reached out, grabbed Duvall's gun, and whispered in his ear. "Hey, she knows this guy. Maybe she can deliver a message to him!"

Duvall smiled. "Hmm, good idea."

He turned to face Emma, who had her hands folded in prayer. "My partner here says you can keep breathing if you deliver a message to JT Thomas."

Emma stopped praying. "Yes, I could do that," she said.

"Okay, here is the message. He needs to meet us at the campsite along the creek a mile south of here. It's a quarter mile from the trail and he can't miss it. Tell him if he turns himself over to us no one else has to die. Except this guy."

He raised his Colt and drilled the clerk in the forehead. The man dropped dead on the floor of the porch.

"Three days, then we come back here every day and kill someone until he has the balls to give himself up."

Duvall turned his horse. "Let's get the hell out of here!" he yelled to the gang.

≈ ≈ ≈ ≈ ≈

Barnabas Poe did, in fact, spend the weekend in the St. Louis jail, but posted bail early Monday morning, vowing never to go back. *My God,* he thought, *I never knew what went on in there. The inmates are disgusting animals! I can't ever tell anyone what happened to me.*

He returned to his office, very aware of the Pinkerton agent following him. He blew by his assistant and slumped down at his desk. He picked up a letter that had been opened by his assistant, which was normal procedure. It was a cease and desist order from the law firm of Tillson, Morrow, and Campbell, but what caught his eye that it was co-addressed to the St. Louis and New York Bar Associations.

Poe called his assistant into his office. She had a frown and a worried look on her face. "Miss Clayton, please take a letter for me. Address it to the law firm of Tillson, Morrow, and Campbell, and send copies to the St. Louis and New York Bar Associations. Tell them we have received their cease and desist letter and we will comply immediately. Furthermore, we are returning the $10,000 bounty to Mr. Marcus Payne along with the $2,000 in legal fees. Also, include that we will have rescinded all agreements with Marcus Payne and Sheriff Xavier Duvall and will have nothing to do with them in the future!"

Miss Clayton looked up. "Sir, we're not supposed to reveal our clients' names!" she exclaimed.

Poe pounded his fist on the desk. "I don't give damn about that. If I don't do this, and do it quickly, I will be disbarred. And you, my friend, will be looking for a new job!"

"I'll get right on it," she said, as she hurried out of the office. *I'll write the damn letter for him*, she thought. *And my letter of resignation as well!*

Chapter Thirteen

JT woke up and made himself a breakfast of bacon and flapjacks. He smiled at the memory of the red-furred cougar. He didn't know why, but he was sure he would see her again. After cleaning up, he tended to his horses and his new mule, then set out to get the deer that had eluded him yesterday.

He returned to where he had thrown the corn the night before and was delighted to see three does eating warily from the pile. JT dropped into a crouch and slowly made his way toward them. Once he had a clear shot, he took careful aim with his Winchester and pulled the trigger. His target dropped immediately to the ground and he smiled. *A clean heart shot. No chasing this meal through the forest!* The other two deer bounded into the woods.

JT gutted and skinned the animal, keeping the loins for his recipe and enough steak to make jerky. He had just finished making a bag from the hide to hold the choice meat when he saw a flash of red in the forest. *Must be that cougar,* he thought. He cut a venison steak for the cat, laid it across the carcass, and headed back to the cabin.

JT had been taught to cook by his parents, and he enjoyed it. He found it relaxing and mind cleansing. He put on an old shirt (he would never be caught dead in an apron) and prepared all the ingredients for venison stew.

First, he cubed the venison loins and seared them in a skillet. He chopped onions, carrots, and potatoes, putting them in a big iron pot with a generous chunk of butter. He mixed in bay leaf, oregano, garlic salt, water, and a bit of flour. Lastly, he added a healthy splash of Worcestershire sauce, a London concoction that had been available in the U.S. since 1839. He tasted a drop on his finger and smiled, recalling how much his father loved it. The man even rubbed it on his head to make his hair grow. JT added the meat, stirred everything together, and covered the pot.

Looking at his watch and seeing that it was nearly five, JT took a bottle of Scotch off the top shelf and poured himself two fingers, adding a drop of water. He began to clean and oil his guns, humming a tune and sniffing the pleasant aroma of the simmering stew. He would have liked some bread, but he had never developed the knack for baking.

When he was finished with his guns and drink, he went to check on Pete and Re-Pete. As he opened the cabin door, he heard a shot and his hat flew off his head. JT closed the door quickly, grabbed his Winchester, and moved to the window. His hat lay on the floor with a neat hole in the crown.

He couldn't see the shooter from the window, but from the corner of his eye he saw a flash of red in the forest. Moments later, a man dashed out of the woods, screaming. JT raised his rifle and was about to shoot when a red-haired cougar closed the distance and jumped on the fleeing man's back. JT watched in awe as the cat brought the man down and grabbed his exposed neck in its powerful jaws. The man tried to pry the cat's mouth open, but it simply squeezed the man's neck tighter and began to shake him back and forth as his strangled screams slowly died.

The cat lowered her catch to the ground and turned toward JT's cabin. She sniffed at the dead hombre, looked once more at the cabin, and bounded back into the woods.

Scanning the woods and seeing no other threats, JT opened the door. He placed his ventilated hat back on his head and walked carefully toward the corpse. The man's face seemed familiar, but he didn't know from where. He stripped him of his holster and pistol, then strode briskly to the spot where he had first seen him. There he found a brand new 50 caliber repeating Winchester and picked it up just as he heard a horse snickering in the forest. He walked over, patted the animal on the neck, and grabbed the reins.

Another horse for old Buck. I guess he really is going to have to start that ranch! And another nice rifle for me.

Chapter Fourteen

Gregor Nelson stayed in St. Louis long enough to get word of Barnabas Poe's response. Drew Morrow heard that the Bar Association was indeed convening their disbarment council. The word was that Poe was not only going to be disbarred for life, but also facing a hefty fine and possible jail time.

Morrow and Nelson met with Marshal Benson and reported the good news. Benson grinned and said, "Let's print up duplicate wanted posters with an X through JT's face, and a declaration that the reward is hereby canceled by order of the governor!"

Gregor nodded. "Great idea, James. And Drew, how about if the Bar Association adds to the fines they have levied so Poe pays for them!"

"Even better," Morrow replied with a chortle. "I will make it happen."

Gregor reached out his hand. "Marshal, you and the governor have been very helpful. Please let us know what we can do for you."

Benson smiled. "Well, another re-election contribution is always appreciated!"

Gregor reached into his pocket, extracted a canvas bag filled with gold coins, and handed it over. "I thought you might say that, so I came prepared!" he said with a laugh. "And now,

I've got a train to catch. Good to know you, and keep up the good work!"

"Vaya con Dios," said Benson, with a tip of his hat.

Gregor and Morrow got into the attorney's carriage and headed for the train to Colorado. They shook hands as Gregor boarded. Morrow assured him that he would keep all concerned informed via wire and letter, and that he would work with Mort Bernstein to seek revenge on the notorious Marcus Payne.

Gregor settled into his compartment with a feeling of contentment. He was looking forward to seeing Emma again, and JT would be happy with the good news.

≈≈≈≈≈

Jean Cantrell went to the livery to retrieve her horses, stopping at the mercantile to supply up for the long ride to JT Thomas's cabin. Her guns were cleaned, oiled, and loaded. She was singing a happy tune as she set out.

Finally, I'll have revenge for Cain's murder. And $10,000 to boot!

The journey was not without glitches. She got turned around and lost more than once and the skies opened up for two days while she huddled under a makeshift lean-to. What she had thought would be a three-day trip ended up taking five days. She was crabby, exhausted, and no longer singing when she finally spotted JT's cabin through the forest. She pulled out an old spyglass that had been her brother's and surveyed JT's cabin. She hadn't eaten since breakfast, and her stomach growled.

If he comes out on the deck, I'll pick him off and help myself to his food.

Jean inched closer to the cabin with growing disappointment. It looked deserted, with no horses tethered in front. Even with the sun shining through the cabin windows, she saw no movement.

Damn, all this way and he isn't even here!

She slithered her way up to the cabin, poked her head up and peered through the window. From what she could see the cabin was empty; it gave off that deserted feeling. She stood up with her Colt in her hand, went to the front door, and carefully tried the latch. The door didn't budge and Jean sighed.

Why does it always have to be difficult?

She raised her pistol and was aiming at the lock when she heard a low growl behind her. The next thing she knew, she was on her back and her gun had flown into the yard. Jean looked up into the flaming eyes of the biggest cougar she had ever seen. She lay frozen as the cat growled again and slowly advanced toward her.

Jean was so terrified she whimpered and soiled her underwear, but she still couldn't move. The cat straddled her and put her head an inch from Jean's nose. Jean closed her eyes and, for the first time since her folks died, prayed to God. The growling stopped, but even with her eyes closed Jean could tell that the cat hadn't moved. She opened one eye, then the other. The cat growled once more and shook its head back and forth, as if to say NO. Then it turned, springing off the cabin porch and running rapidly into the woods. Before the wild beast disappeared, it looked over its shoulder and growled loudly one more time before disappearing into the dense forest.

Jean lay on the cabin deck for nearly ten minutes, whimpering. She stood up on trembling legs and looked at the locked door. Then she sighed and made her way down the stairs, picking up her Colt and cautiously making her way into the woods. She sensed that the cat was gone, but she took no chances until she found her horse, mounted, and took off in a canter.

Jean looked over her shoulder at the cabin and headed back toward Point Stevens Pass, her hunger forgotten and her pants in need of a wash.

≈≈≈≈≈

JT woke up after a good night's sleep. He had buried the shooter the night before and spent the evening eating a big bowl of stew and thinking about the red-furred cougar.

My God, is that Annabelle coming back to protect me? Naw, that couldn't be. Or could it?

He was still full, so he skipped breakfast and tended to the horses and mule. Putting his remaining supplies in the mule's deep saddlebags, he saddled up Pete and Re-Pete. After making sure the cabin was in order and locked up, he mounted up and headed for Point Stevens Pass. He had been gone for eight days, and he wanted to get there ahead of Gregor Nelson.

Once he arrived, he was surprised to see men on the rooftops with rifles. The closest one recognized JT, waving and calling out to the other marksmen. "It's okay—it's JT!"

What the hell happened while I was gone? JT wondered.

Chapter Fifteen

Tim Yates rode back into camp with a lot on his mind. The rest of the gang was in high spirits, and Duvall was especially jovial. "My God, that lippy clerk talked himself right into an early grave. Did you see the look on his face before I shot him? I think he shit himself!" he said, laughing.

Tim nodded and frowned, making no comment. Perez, on the other hand, laughed and slapped Duvall on the backside. "Now I know why Marcus Payne took to you, Xavier. That was a thing of beauty!"

Duvall smiled and told Tim to take care of their horses. "Now, let's go get a drink!" he said to Perez.

"Just one? Hell, we got three days to drink and eat before we kill Mr. JT Thomas or one of the town folk," Perez bellowed, as he headed for the tent with the whiskey.

Duvall followed him. "Oh, I know exactly who I'm going to kill. That gal who said she knew JT. But first, I'm bringing her back here and having some fun with her!"

Perez nodded his approval. "Not a bad idea. I'll go second, and then you can turn her over to the deputies. I'm thinking after they are finished with her you won't even need to kill her!"

Tim Yates was in shock as he tended to the horses.

Oh my God, this is awful. How the hell did I get mixed up with these guys?

≈ ≈ ≈ ≈ ≈

The armed men on the rooftops saw Gregor arrive and passed the word from rooftop to rooftop until JT was notified. Gregor dismounted in front of the hotel, and JT hurried down the steps to meet him. "What the hell is going on here?" Gregor exclaimed.

JT frowned. "It's not good. A gang came in two days ago and surrounded the hotel. They rounded everyone up and said they were looking for me. I wasn't here, so they shot the hotel clerk!"

"Son of a bitch! Are you kidding me?"

"Oh no, I'm not. They said if I didn't meet them at the campsite outside of town they would come back and shoot someone else!"

Gregor looked up at the armed men on the rooftops. "Hmm. So, they gave you a warning and designated the spot? These guys are not terribly bright, are they?"

JT smiled for the first time since returning. "They aren't, but you never know what they have up their sleeves. I'm told there were quite a few of them, and that campsite is so densely forested they could set up an ambush and get away scot-free!"

Gregor nodded. "Maybe, but they'll have to get close enough for a clean shot if they want to collect on your sorry butt! Anyway, I need to get checked in and cleaned up. How about meeting me at the saloon in half an hour?"

JT nodded. "Sounds good to me."

"Oh, by the way, I have good news from St. Louis. I'll tell you over that drink as long as you're buying."

When Gregor walked into the Stevens Saloon, a new bartender greeted him. "What can I get you?" he asked.

Gregor nodded at the beer spigots. "A lager, please, and a Kentucky whiskey on the side."

"Coming right up."

He set the warm beer down on the bar with a flourish. Gregor lifted it to his lips and downed half the glass with his eyes closed. "Oh, that is tasty," he sighed. "You're new here, aren't you?"

"Yep, first day," the bartender replied.

"No offense, but what happened to Adrian? Did he go to work at his brother Buffalo's saloon?"

"No, he just didn't show up for work."

JT pushed through the saloon doors, made his way to the old walnut bar, and slapped Gregor on the back. "I see you got started without me," he said with a chuckle.

"Yep, and I ain't paid for it either," Gregor said with a wide grin.

JT greeted the new bartender. "Hello. Who are you, and where is Adrian?"

The man smiled. "Like I just told your friend, he didn't show up for work, so here I am. What can I get you?"

"I'll have what he is having, and get him another round."

As JT pulled up a barstool, it suddenly dawned on him.

The guy who tried to ambush me at the cabin, the one the cat killed—that was Adrian! God darn, no wonder he looked familiar. And I bet he overheard DeWitt giving directions to my cabin.

Gregor looked at JT. "What's on your mind? Looks like you've seen a ghost."

"Not a ghost, just a corpse and a cougar," JT replied.

"What are you talking about?"

"Gregor, do you believe in reincarnation?"

"Why, I never thought about it. I don't think so, but how the hell would I know?"

"Yeah, me either. Now, my mother is convinced that my father was reincarnated as a bird. When she sees a cardinal, she talks to it like it was my father."

"Well, maybe she's right and we are wrong. But what harm does it do, especially if the cardinal gives her good advice!"

"I hadn't thought about that! Oh well, we have bigger fish to fry in any case. We can't let those outlaws come back into town and shoot someone on my account."

"No, we certainly can't. These folks have a life to live and they can't be standing on the rooftops forever," Gregor replied.

JT stared into the mirror in silence for several long minutes. Then he nodded to himself, threw back the rest of his whiskey, and smiled.

"My friend, I'm going out to that damn campsite and I'm going to turn the tables on these assholes," he stated. "I'm going to ambush them. Then I'm going to head up the mountain away from Point Stevens Pass and give whoever survives the chase of their lives!"

"You sure about that?" Gregor asked.

"Oh, yeah." JT grinned. "Now, what's your good news?"

≈ ≈ ≈ ≈ ≈

As Gregor finished telling his St. Louis story over supper, JT gave him a thumbs up. "Gregor, that is outstanding!"

Gregor smiled. "Well, I had a lot of help, and this Attorney Poe had pretty much hung himself with his latest escapade."

"I should say so," JT said with a smirk. "Say, I've been thinking. Why don't we start our own detective agency? From what I hear, those damn Pinkertons are raising hell with the unions from New York to Chicago, and I can't abide by that!"

Gregor looked up at JT. "By God, if you mean it, that's a fine idea. My father was in a union and it always grated on me that the Pinks aligned themselves with the robber barons! I'm in, and I'm sure I can bring over at least a dozen like-minded people."

"Oh, I'm serious. Reach out and get those guys here as fast as you can. I want you to lead them in defending Point Stevens Pass while I'm gone."

"Consider it done! Shall we drink to our new venture?"

Gregor and JT clinked their glasses together, smiling. Then Gregor turned serious and said, "But don't you want some help out there? There are a lot of those guys, and they probably don't know that the reward has been rescinded."

JT finished his drink. "Oh, I'm sure for one of them the money won't make any difference. For Sheriff Duvall and me, this is personal."

JT stopped at the mercantile and picked up enough food for a week in the mountains. He also bought plenty of ammunition and a large bundle of dynamite. The clerk put the supplies in JT's saddlebags. "You starting a war, Mr. JT?" he asked with a laugh.

JT grinned. "No, but I'll surely end one if I'm pushed into it!"

He headed to the livery, where he greeted Buck. He gave his horses and mule an apple and said, "Buck, I'm headed out to face those outlaws. I'd like to leave my horses here, and I would like to take my mule with me. If you have an old nag that has seen better days, I'll take that as well. This ought to cover it," he said, as he tossed a gold piece over.

Buck smiled as he pocketed the coin. "Sure, I've got one. She was actually going to the saloon to make steaks and stew, but she's yours now. Her name is Nelly, and I've kind of grown attached to her, so please take her!"

JT nodded. "Throw an old saddle on her while I pack up the mule. I need to move along."

Buck saddled Nelly and handed JT the reins. "Good luck to you, my friend. Watch your back and kill those sons of bitches!"

JT headed out to the campsite at as brisk a pace as Nelly and the mule could manage. After carefully surveying the deserted campsite and the surrounding forest, he made his way to the old fire pit. He dismounted and tied the animals to a tree, then spread out an extra bedroll stuffed with blankets. He also took his old hat with the bullet hole in it and set it at the top of the bedroll. Then he lit a small fire, took out a note, and placed it on a stone near the fire pit.

Duvall,

I know it was you that killed the hotel clerk and I damn well know it was Marcus Payne that put the bounty on my head. I'm coming for you, but first I'd like to show you the Colorado mountains. They are beautiful this time of year. So head west, and I'll leave a few signs to point you in the right direction. As to the rest of your scuzzy crew, this is their last chance to turn around and head home. After today, I'll shoot them on sight.

Disrespectfully Yours,

John Thurgood Thomas

P.S. The wanted poster has been squashed, and Barnabas Poe is in jail!

JT smiled as he stood and led his mule up toward the mountain. He looked at the blue sky, pulled his winter coat around him, and chuckled.

No more hiding out at the cabin, I'm taking the offensive!

Chapter Sixteen

Duvall surveyed the camp on the creek with his spyglass. His men were spread out in the woods, all armed with rifles and anxious to collect their part of the $10,000. He saw a horse tethered to a tree and the smoke from a small campfire. He also saw what he assumed to be a sleeping man in a bedroll with a hat covering his face. Duvall looked at Pérez and handed him the spyglass. "What the hell is that? Why would JT be sleeping this early in his bedroll?"

"It ain't him," Pérez replied. "Could be some other drifter, and maybe he's sick or something."

"That could be, but if that's the case this is his unlucky day." Duvall raised his Winchester and hollered "FIRE!" The forest echoed with rifle fire and the bedroll jumped as bullets tore it up. Duvall took one more shot and held his rifle up over his head. "Enough, stop firing. He's dead!" He let out a whoop and moved toward the camp.

Duvall dismounted ten feet from the bedroll and shot once more into it. "God damn," he said as he got closer. "That ain't JT Thomas. Hell, it's just blankets and a bedroll!"

The rest of the gang drifted in from the woods, and Duvall noticed the note on the rock. He knelt down and read it, getting redder and redder in the face. Pérez moved up next to him, trying to look over his shoulder. "What's that?" he inquired.

Duvall squeezed his eyes shut and looked up at the sky. "It's a note from that damn JT Thomas. He's calling us out. We're supposed to head west, and he will point us in the right direction if we need it!" he said, and threw the note in the fire.

"Is that all it said?" Pérez asked, as he watched the letter go up in smoke.

"No, he said this is the last warning and he will shoot anyone on sight. And if it's worth $10,000, then keep coming!" Duvall replied.

Duvall looked around at the ragtag group. "Anyone want to back out now?" he bellowed out.

The men called out. "Not me." "Not me." "I'm in." "I can taste the money now."

Only Tim Yates did not answer. *Son of a buckshot. Shot on sight?*

≈ ≈ ≈ ≈ ≈

JT headed up the mountain, leading his sure-footed mule. "Mule, if we're going to hang out for a while, I best give you a name. Any suggestions?" The mule continued to follow JT and did not respond. "Hmm, cat got your tongue? Okay, I guess it's up to me. You're brown, so I guess we could call you Brown." With that, the mule stopped. "What, you don't like that name? How about Dirt Brown?" The mule looked

JT in the eye but didn't move an inch. JT tugged the rope. "Damn, mule, we need to get going. You sure are stubborn!" The mule nodded his head and moved ahead. "Well, I'll be damned," JT said as he continued up the mountainside. "Stubborn it is. Hell, that's a good name for a mule!"

JT stopped intermittently and broke branches on a few trees to help the posse find the way. He stopped just before dark and made a cold camp, no fire. He chewed on his stash of venison jerky and took a slug out of his canteen. As darkness settled around him, he rolled himself into his new bedroll, covered himself with a new blanket, and covered his face with his new Stetson. He also took the unique revolver out of its holster and placed it on his chest. He fell into a light dozing sleep, alert to the night sounds.

At dawn, JT watered the mule and gave him a hatful of oats. "I bet no one has ever given you oats before," he said. "You look like a hay mule." Stubborn stared ahead with no response as he ate. "You're not much of a talker, are you, Mr. Stubborn? Okay then, let's get going. I have a little surprise planned for you."

As they made their way up the mountain, JT was delighted with the sure-footed mule. Pete and Re-Pete would not have been able to make the climb, and JT doubted the posse's horses could either. He pushed right through the noon hour, stopping just long enough to eat a strip of jerky and give Stubborn a hatful of water. In the late afternoon, he stopped in a level spot that was hidden from the view below by large boulders. He tethered Stubborn, fed and watered him, and prepared the camp for an overnight stay.

JT gingerly took out three sticks of dynamite from his saddlebags, rolled them in a shirt, and stuffed them in the bottom of a leather pouch. He added some jerky, his canteen, and a box of shells. He lifted the bag's strap over his shoulder, settled it on his hip, and grabbed his Winchester. "You look after the camp, Mr. Stubborn," he told the mule. "I'll be back after dark."

JT backtracked for a half mile and stopped at the spot he had passed earlier—a perfect spot for an ambush. Laying his rifle down, he took the shells out and lined them up. He got the food, water, and matches out, then carefully removed the dynamite and set it aside. He stuffed the empty bag into a crevice between two small boulders to steady his aim. His ambush spot now ready, he sat with his back against a warm boulder and dozed a bit, keeping one eye open.

The sun feels good, even if the air is a bit chilly. Nothing to do now but wait.

≈ ≈ ≈ ≈ ≈

Gregor Nelson met up with the sheriff of Point Stevens Pass, Tad Dowling. Tad wasn't a real sheriff, just a Stevens' ranch cowpuncher who happened to be a decent shot with a Colt or a Winchester. Tad had stepped into the slot at Lewis Stevens' insistence. Stevens was the founder of Point Stevens Pass. He owned more than half of the shops, the bank, and the largest saloon. His daughter's husband, the former sheriff and Tad's drinking buddy, had been killed in a bank robbery. Tad acted not only out of loyalty, but because he was sweet on Stevens' daughter and thought an act of courage and honor might help win her over.

They headed over to the empty hotel café, where they met with four Pinkertons. Gregor had brought the Pinks, as they were called, up to speed on what had been happening in town. He also laid out JT's proposal to start a new agency to compete with the Pinks. He told them he wanted them each to serve as team leaders, reporting to himself, with JT as the ultimate boss. He explained how rich JT was, and told the story about the cave, the rescue, and New York.

All four had immediately accepted, especially when he told them about the salary they would receive and the fact that they would focus on real bad guys with bounties on their heads instead of honest union men. Each smiled when Gregor told them they would keep the bulk of the reward in addition to their annual salary.

Gregor leaned toward the men. "The job at hand is to protect Point Stevens Pass and its residents. Any nonresidents will not be allowed to carry a firearm. I want a man at each end of Main Street. Any outsiders will either be relieved of their guns, sent packing, or shot; not necessarily in that order!"

"Sheriff Tad will make additional rounds from sunup to sundown with an additional new deputy," he added. "The two remaining men will move from saloon to saloon, catching any strangers that have slipped through the cracks. I'll lend support as needed. My plan is to nap during the day and make rounds after dark."

One of the men spoke up. "I know some more Pinkertons who'd love to join up. Why don't I get them to replace the posters throughout Colorado? Then they can meet us here."

Gregor agreed immediately and smiled at the men.

This may work, and thank God I don't need to return to New York City!

Chapter Seventeen

Duvall's gang headed west toward the mountains, Winchesters at the ready. There was an air of excitement throughout the ranks. Pérez led the pack, but to his chagrin Duvall hung back, making the excuse that he needed to watch their back trail. They finally got to the mountains and the smiles left their faces as they rode single file up the steep trail. As the way got steeper, the inexperienced horses began to slip and slide, their riders falling to the hard ground. As dusk approached, one long-haired man ended up in a prickly bush as his horse turned tail and headed down the mountain. Pulling thorns out of his backside and swearing, he called for help as he chased after it.

Just then, a shot rang out. The outlaws quickly threw themselves to the ground, taking any cover they could find. Duvall turned his horse and rode quickly down the mountain.

Pérez, on the other hand, was still seated on his horse. The horse was standing in place, quivering and snorting. Pérez's Winchester was in his hands, which were frozen shut. Blood poured from his neck, soaking his shirt and the horse. Above the neck was nothing but empty space.

The outlaws burrowed even farther into their hidey-holes, glancing up at their long-time leader, minus his ugly head.

Tim Yates looked up, then turned his head and vomited.

Holy shit, what have I gotten myself into!

≈ ≈ ≈ ≈ ≈

Moments after he squeezed the trigger and watched the lead rider's head disintegrate into brains, flesh, and blood, JT realized with disappointment that the victim wasn't Xavier Duvall. He stuffed the extra cartridges back into his leather pouch, then carefully picked up the nearest stick of dynamite. He kissed it with a smile, held it out at arm's length, and lit it.

He threw it a bit ahead of where the riders had stopped. He quickly picked up another, lit it, and threw it a bit farther. He grabbed the last stick, lit it, and threw it as far as he could. The three explosions threw dirt, rocks, and small boulders into the air and started a small avalanche. *Well, I certainly got their attention!* JT laughed, quickly gathered his belongings, and headed back to his new buddy Stubborn.

It was pitch black as he slowly made his way back to camp. JT stopped every ten feet or so and lit a match, careful that it wouldn't be seen from below. With the final match he spotted Stubborn, standing and sniffing the air. *Hmm, he knows match sulfur.*

He quickly built a small fire and made dinner with the leftover venison loins seasoned with onion salt, paprika, and coarse pepper. He ate out of the hot skillet, foregoing a plate. Afterward, he threw more wood on the fire, cleaned up after himself as best he could and decided he needed to celebrate. Retrieving the Scotch, he poured two fingers into his coffee cup and held it to the sky.

One down at least!

≈ ≈ ≈ ≈ ≈

Tim Yates was frozen to the spot, shaking with fear and trying not to look up.

Rocks and dirt had been falling on him, and a boulder had nearly decapitated him. His so-called buddies were starting to get up from their hiding places. A few were moaning and whimpering.

Good, they deserve it, they brought it on themselves. Me too.

Duvall rode back up the mountain and rejoined the dusty, dirty outlaw gang. He stared at Pérez's headless corpse. "Thomas is going to pay for this, in spades," he said grimly. "Right now, let's get back down the mountain. We need to regroup and catch up with this animal tomorrow."

The outlaw gang made their way down the mountain, licking their wounds. Tim gathered the horses that hadn't bolted and wondered if he should simply slip out in the middle of the night. He shuddered, remembering the headless Pérez.

On the other hand, this JT Thomas is still worth $10,000, and he most certainly is a killer!

≈ ≈ ≈ ≈ ≈

Gregor Nelson had walked around Point Stevens Pass for two days and was getting antsy. The moon was shining bright with the whisper of a cloud overhead. No one was moving, and his new agents had pretty much shut down the town to drifters and strangers. He thought about JT. Since none of the gang of outlaws had come back to town, Gregor was pretty sure they were chasing JT through the mountains. He scratched his chin and thought about how he could help.

Perhaps I should check out his cabin. Doctor DeWitt knows the directions, and JT might be sheltering there from his pursuers. My men will welcome JT if he comes back to town. But the cabin—would he really be safe there?

≈ ≈ ≈ ≈ ≈

Jean rode out of Redstone, Colorado, freshly supplied with money from the livery owner who had needed some womanly attention. Unfortunately for him, he had flashed a large roll of bills as he paid her off and Jean slit his throat with a dozen onlookers. Lucky for her, horses made poor witnesses.

She was headed for JT Thomas's cave. JT had pointed out the area during the initial ride to Point Stevens Pass. Jean had no idea where JT was, but she sure as hell wasn't going back to his cabin with that guardian cougar around. She shuddered just thinking about it.

The ride was uneventful, and before long she spotted the turn-off. Jean kneed her horse in the flanks but was cut off by three riders. She quickly slid her sawed-off Greener shotgun out of its scabbard and pointed it at the closest Indian. He was clothed in nothing but a loincloth, in spite of the chilly weather.

She smiled but didn't say a word. The Indian made a placating gesture, indicating that she should stop and put down her weapon. Jean nodded and began to lower the Greener. The brave smiled and nodded. Jean grinned as well, then quickly raised the gun and blew the man out of the saddle. The brave on his left raised his old dilapidated muzzleloader, and Jean laughed as she took careful aim at his head and blew his brains out.

The remaining man, armed only with a bow, turned and ran away. Jean slid her Winchester out of its scabbard and took careful aim. She deliberately shot the brave's horse, then galloped toward the man, now pinned under the fallen animal.

She dismounted, keeping the Winchester trained on the struggling brave. His legs were pinned. Jean chuckled, then shot the horse through the head. Jean looked at the brave pinned under the dead horse. She knocked the Indian in the middle of his forehead with the butt of the Winchester, then removed his bow and arrows and a knife he had tied around his waist.

She leaned down close to the man's face. "You know, I've heard lots of stories about how you treat white women when you capture them. Like skinning them alive and burning, too. Maybe you would like a taste of your own medicine!"

The man's knife was old and shabby, but it was still mighty sharp. She began to cut pine branches off the trees near the trail, piling them next to the dead horse. She gathered dry brush and dead wood, piled it on the Indian and the horse, then topped the pile with more pine branches.

She dug into her saddlebags and pulled out Cain's last bottle of Scotch with a smile. Digging a bit deeper, she found matches. She returned to the brave, who was now feebly moving around. He was chanting and had a grimace on his face.

Jean bent down and took a swig of the Scotch. She half-heartedly offered the bottle to the Indian, then pulled back. "Oops, whiskey ain't good for Indians, is it? Well, more for me."

She sprinkled a bit of the whiskey on a dry mound of wood and took out a long match. She held in front of the still chanting Indian and grinned from ear to ear. "You know, I've never burned someone alive before. My brother Cain did that, and I missed all the fun!" Jean said, taking one more swig of whiskey. She lit the match, dropped it on the whiskey-soaked wood, and stepped back as the flames licked high into the air. The brave stopped chanting and let out a deathly scream.

Jean tilted her back and howled. "Now that's more like it!" she yelled maniacally.

Chapter Eighteen

JT woke up after a surprisingly good night's sleep and surveyed the mountain slope for creeping outlaws. After tending to the mule, which he was starting to grow fond of, he had a nice breakfast and a quick washup. He broke camp, making sure to leave signs of his recent presence, and headed for a dense forest of evergreens about a quarter mile ahead.

He climbed up on the mule and kneed him in the ribs, heading toward the forest. Stubborn took off like a bat out of hell, and JT was forced to hold on to the mule's mane since he had no saddle. The mule ran into the forest and headed straight for the trunk of a huge pine. JT was about to bail out when Stubborn stopped inches from a collision—then snorted and collapsed to the ground. Dead before he hit the dirt.

Holy shit! JT thought, his legs spread wide on the mule. He dusted himself off, then stood up and retrieved his guns and the heavy saddlebags. *Well, this changes everything. I need a new plan!*

Looking behind him, he ascertained that no one was chasing him. He sat on the still-warm mule and looked at his surroundings, his mind racing. *What's at hand, and how can I make it work for me?*

Sad as it was, his new buddy Stubborn was now nothing but meat, and he had no desire to add that meat to the posse's supplies. Sighing, he got his Bowie knife and quickly started in on the mule. He took the ruined heart from the chest cavity and butchered the loins. Then he flayed a bit of hide to wrap them in and put the meat in the saddlebag.

JT dragged the saddlebag to a distant spot behind a thick tree trunk and removed a stick of dynamite. He returned and grimaced as he inserted it into the mule's heart cavity, pulled out a match and lit the fuse. He ran back into the forest and lay flat behind the widest tree he could find, closed his eyes, and put his hands over his ears.

Moments later, he heard and smelled the explosion. He waited for a minute, then poked his head around the pine tree. There was a large hole in the ground that was still smoking. Whatever was left of Stubborn was fair game for the crows and worms.

JT shook his head. *Hell of a way to go, Stubborn.*

He smiled as he looked at the crater the explosion had made, then took his Bowie knife and cut a dozen or more pine branches. He trimmed them, shortened them to about twelve inches, and sharpened them at one end. He pounded the sharp stakes into the firm ground at the bottom of the hole, climbed out, and placed larger pine boughs over the crater. He then trimmed branches off the trees, making a path from the pit to the edge of the forest. There, he slashed arrows into the ground, pointing the way. He knew that the mule's last gallop had left enough of a trail, but he wasn't taking any chances.

JT headed back, hiding his saddlebags and Winchester about a quarter mile into the forest. Near the pit, he chewed on some jerky, sat down, and waited patiently.

≈ ≈ ≈ ≈ ≈

Xavier Duvall woke up with a hangover and two wounded deputies as a result of JT's dynamite. Tim Yates had a fire going and was helping the cook, Olen Thompson, who was one of the injured. Slowly, the gang got up from their bedrolls and blankets, having sniffed the coffee and bacon. Duvall could not make out what was being said, but he heard grumbling and cursing. He hardly knew Pérez and he certainly didn't miss him, but these men who had ridden with him were now without a leader. That had to change, and fast.

He got up and put on his hat, handing his breakfast plate to Tim. Then he pulled out his Colt and fired one shot into the air. All of the men looked up as he yelled, "Come on over to the fire pit. I need to talk to you." The men slowly drifted over, standing in groups or sitting on boulders.

"I know you all are mourning Sheriff Pérez. You all had ridden with him for a long time. From what I could tell, he was a good leader and was fair with all of you. But… he is gone and we need to continue this search." Duvall paused as he heard grumbling. "I know, I know," he acknowledged. "But here is the deal: I will pay you each one hundred dollars now, and another one thousand dollars each when we catch and kill JT Thomas!"

Most of the outlaws smiled broadly, but one scruffy mountain of a man with a two-gun rig stepped forward. "So, you got all this money in your saddlebags, Mr. Xavier Duvall?"

Duvall deftly slipped his hammer strap off and looked the man in the eye. "Why do you ask?"

"Well, 'cause maybe we take the money now and send you to hell."

Without warning, Duvall drew his Colt and drilled the rabble-rouser in the forehead. The man fell backwards into the fire and landed on the large coffee pot.

Duvall looked around. Most of the men were looking at the tops of their boots. "Anyone else want to try?"

Everyone shook their heads. Xavier twirled his fancy Colt twice before he slid it into his black leather holster. "Okay then, line up and get you your hundred dollars. Then we will get after that damn JT Thomas. The days a-wastin'."

Tim collected his hundred dollars, then went to start a new pot of coffee.

I need to get the hell out of here!

Gregor Nelson made his way to JT's cabin after getting
directions from Doctor DeWitt. It was starting to get cold at
night and chilly during the day. The colorful leaves were no
longer on the trees but under foot. There was a smell of
winter in the air, and while Gregor was new to Colorado, he
sensed that snow was right around the corner. But the view
was beautiful and the forest quiet, certainly not like New
York City.

He arrived at the cabin and dismounted in front of the deck,
then made his way up the stairs and knocked on the door.
He tried the latch and found it was locked, so he peered
through the nearest window. There was no one in the cabin,
but it was neat and tidy with numerous pots and pans
hanging on the wall above the stove. Gregor knew JT would
not mind if he broke in, but he didn't feel right about it. He
decided to stay a while, and if JT didn't show up in a few days
he would head to the cave.

$$\approx \approx \approx \approx \approx$$

Tim Yates brought up the rear with orders to holler out if he
spotted JT Thomas. Duvall was leading the gang back toward
the mountain when he stopped and looked at fresh mule
tracks that veered off into a pine forest. He held up his hand.
"Follow me, but keep an eye out. This may be another
ambush," he ordered. Following the tracks as they headed

into the woods, he spotted JT's markers pointing the way. "God damn him," he growled to himself.

He put up a hand, and the gang gathered around. He took out two fifty-dollar gold pieces, holding them over his head. "I need two volunteers to follow these tracks!" he said. Two men raised their hands and Duvall handed them the coins. "Be careful, and holler if you see him. We will wait right here for your signal."

The two outlaws made their way slowly into the forest, hardly noticing the alley that JT had cut through the woods. As they approached the pit, JT stepped out from behind a tree some forty yards away. "Hey," he yelled at the top of his voice, "I'm over here, assholes. Come and get me!" He turned around and quickly disappeared into the forest.

The lead man spurred his horse into a gallop, protecting himself by ducking behind the animal's head. As a result, he didn't even see the pine-covered pit, but the horse certainly did. He jumped over it, bucking the man off his back. The outlaw crashed through the pine boughs and screamed as he was impaled on the sharp spikes.

The second man slowly approached the pit with his rifle raised, expecting an ambush. He dismounted and looked at his pal, then turned his head and threw up his breakfast. The bloody hombre tried to speak, but he simply gurgled blood and spit. He was speared through the calf, his right arm, his left buttock, and his right ear. The final, lethal spike was right through his stomach. "Shoot me, Jack, God damn it! Please shoot me!" he exclaimed in agony.

Jack raised his shaking Winchester, sweat trickling down his face. He lowered it and looked at his friend. "God damn it do it, now, please!' his wounded friend whispered. Jack raised his rifle again and took careful aim. "See you in hell, my friend," he said, as he put a bullet into the man's nose. Then he mounted his horse, turned around, and looked back to where the gang was waiting. He put his Winchester back in the scabbard and turned into the woods, away from them.

That's it for me, I'm out of here. JT Thomas and $10,000 be damned! I'm headed south to the New Mexico Territory, where it's warm and the towns don't have any lawmen.

Chapter Nineteen

Gregor was tired of waiting at JT's cabin. His gut told him that he wasn't coming back soon. He now believed JT was in the mountains, leading the gang of outlaws on a wild goose chase. *You know, that would be kind of fun, as long as you didn't get shot!*

He stood up, thinking about heading back to Point Stevens Pass, where Emma could give him a home-cooked meal and a little comfort as well. But instead, he sighed and headed toward JT's cave. He knew it was a long shot, but he would feel guilty if he were getting a warm meal and womanly comforts while his boss was being pursued by an outlaw posse. *I'll just stick my head in and see if he is there. If not, I'll head back to Point Stevens Pass.*

Pushing the horse and spending long hours in the saddle, Gregor made the trip in record time. He headed for the cave's back entrance, knowing there was grass and water there. When he arrived, he tethered his horse near the mountain stream in a small patch of dying grass. With his Winchester in his hand and his saddlebags over his shoulder, he hiked up the gentle hill toward the cave.

A few yards inside the entrance, he tripped over a lantern. He bent down and picked it up. There was still kerosene in it, so he lit it and moved on, making his way up the long tunnel toward the front entrance.

Midway through the side of the cave that had been hidden by furniture, he saw what the mining expert had described. The wall was seamed with gold. Gregor stopped, putting the lantern on the ground. He took his knife, scraped nearly a quarter of an ounce of gold dust into his hand, and smiled.

Brushing off his hand, he picked up the lantern and made his way to the entrance. As he got close, he saw the drill and pyramid of dynamite the mining men had left. There was sunshine at the opening, and he blew out the lantern. The cave was empty. No JT, and no outlaws.

Gregor's stomach growled as he looked at the fire pit that was already laid and ready to go. *What the heck, if you don't eat you die.* He took the fixings out of his saddlebags, lit the fire, and made himself a decent meal.

He was just finishing up as he heard a horse snicker. He jumped up, grabbed the lantern and his Winchester, and moved back into the darkness of the cave. *Could be JT, or could be the men hunting him. But I'm not taking any chances!*

JT ran up the mountain as quickly as he could, expecting pursuit. He slid backward on the slick hillside a few times, so he slowed down a bit and picked out dry footholds. He soon arrived at his saddlebags and rifle, quickly picked them up, and made his way farther up the mountain.

Stopping behind a large boulder, he took the time to see what was behind him. There was no one in sight, so he continued upwards, trying to put distance between the gang and himself. The climb was grueling, but as dusk slowly crept up the side of the mountain, he finally rested. Ahead on the right was a flat spot with boulders for protection, a good place to park his weary body. JT dragged himself up and collapsed next to a medium-sized boulder with a view of the downslope.

Lord, that was exhausting. I'm not as young as I used to be!

Duvall heard a rifle shot and signaled to his men to get down and be quiet. They waited for several minutes, then carefully ventured into the woods. Duvall stopped short, sniffing the air. "That's blood," he said to no one in particular.

One of the men moved toward the pit, then his horse stopped abruptly and began to back up. "Whoa, we got a pit here!" the man cried out. A few of the gang dismounted and edged up to the hole. One pulled out a match from his pocket, scratched it on a rock, and held it up over the pit. He gasped as he looked down on his fellow outlaw. "God damn, that's Arie down there, and he is as dead as a doornail."

"Is Jack down there too?" Duvall asked.

"Nope, he ain't," the man replied.

Duvall looked warily around at the dense woods. "Let's get out of here," he said, as he turned his horse around and headed back to the forest edge.

As his gang made camp, mumbling and cursing under their breath, Duvall went to his saddlebags, pulled out two bottles of Kentucky whiskey and passed them around. "Let's make camp here and get some dinner and this fine whiskey in our bellies. We'll head after that damned killer in the morning!"

The outlaws all nodded and went about their assigned duties. After a somber dinner, they finished off the whiskey and sacked out for the night, taking their guns to bed with them.

In the morning they set out through the forest, past the dead body of Arie. Some of the outlaws made the sign of the cross as they passed the pit. Tim Yates stopped and looked at the bloody body with no nose. "Aren't we going to bury him?"

"Hell no," said the man next to him. "Hey, critters got to eat too and nobody cottoned to Arie that much. Let him lie like he is."

Another gang member spoke up. "Looks like his chickenshit buddy Jumping Jack skedaddled."

Again, Tim thought about turning tail and heading back to Point Stevens Pass. *Maybe I could learn to love to cut hair. Naw, the more men we lose, the bigger my share gets. And hell, being a barber is damn near like being dead.*

Chapter Twenty

Jean rode carefully up the narrow, twisting mountain trail. As she turned the corner, she spotted the place where JT had shot Cain's cohorts and freed the women. The remains of two horses and men still lay where they fell. Not that she gave a damn about them; they were Cain's buddies, not hers.

Jean kneed her horse in the flank and moved ahead slowly, taking out her Winchester and preparing to end JT Thomas's life if he was in the cave. As she made the last turn and rounded a huge boulder, she spotted a small campfire inside the cave entrance. She moved the rifle barrel back and forth, hoping for a shot at her nemesis. But there was only smoke and air, no JT. She sat patiently while her horse pawed the ground and snickered. Finally, she slid off her saddle and made her way slowly to the cave entrance.

Inside, she spotted a saddlebag, a cast iron skillet smoking in the fire, and the largest drill she had ever seen. Nearby was a lantern and a pyramid of dynamite that brought a smile to her lips. She called out, "I know you're in there, Mr. JT Thomas, and you're going to pay for killing my brother Cain! And yes, I know the reward is no longer being offered but I don't care! I've got you trapped and I'm going to blow you to hell and back!" she exclaimed. "What do you say about that?"

Gregor stood in the dark with his sidearm out, listening. *So, it's Jean Cantrell.* He smiled at her mistaking him for JT, and smiled even more when she said she had him trapped. Gregor knew she was a wanted woman, and JT would be forever grateful if he brought her to justice.

But the comment about blowing him up gave him pause. Gregor responded, trying to imitate JT's voice. "Yeah, you caught me, and your brother deserved to die. How about if we negotiate this and you turn yourself in?" Not waiting for an answer, he then moved quickly toward the rear entrance, anxious to get out into the fresh air and away from the dynamite.

Jean laughed out loud. "Are you crazy, turn myself in? You're gonna die in this miserable cave. I just hope you have to suffer for days first!"

She triggered her Winchester into the dark of the cave, laughing wildly. Dropping to the floor next to the dynamite, she grabbed the lantern and opened the filler cap. Backing her way outside, she emptied it in a line that stretched to the first bend in the winding trail, where she retrieved and mounted her horse. "Go to hell, JT Thomas!" she screamed, as she dropped a match into the kerosene. Then she rode as quickly as she could down the mountain trail, with a grin of delight on her face.

≈ ≈ ≈ ≈ ≈

JT Thomas headed up the mountain at first light, thinking about how he would deal with the outlaws today. He knew he had put a dent in them, perhaps causing some of them to rethink the whole adventure. But even though he really didn't know Xavier Duvall well, he didn't think he would turn around. JT knew the man was not only at the beck and call of Marcus Payne, but that he was being bankrolled by him as well. *No, they won't give up, not at this point, at least.*

As he climbed slowly, he realized he might have to kill them all. He knew he had limited supplies. Stubborn's meat was good for a little while more, but he couldn't hunt or shoot while the gang chased him. In a few days he would be down to cans of peaches and beans.

He stopped and looked to his left and an idea popped into his head. *Maybe, just maybe, I can disrupt the gang.* Perhaps he could let them go by and bring up the rear. They were pretty spread out the last time they followed him, trying to avoid being picked off *en masse*. JT moved off the deer path he had been following and hid.

≈ ≈ ≈ ≈ ≈

Gregor made it to the end of the cave tunnel, moving to the side and away from the entrance. He put his fingers in his ears just before the loudest explosion he had ever heard made him flinch. After a moment, he took his fingers out of his ears and peeked inside. The cave was even darker than before. He picked up the lantern and made his way into the darkness. The first thirty yards was undisturbed, but the next ten had rocks scattered intermittently. Farther inside, the cave floor was littered with small, medium, and large stones and eventually became unnavigable. Lifting the lantern and looking ahead, he could see the cave was completely blocked.

Well, Cantrell would have been right. I would have died in here but for the rear exit.

The lantern picked up a glint and he crouched down, picking up a small rock. It was seamed with gold. Gregor laughed, holding the lantern out in front of him. The cave-blocking pile of rock was gleaming in the lantern light.

Gold! Lots and lots of gold!

≈ ≈ ≈ ≈ ≈

Xavier Duvall led his band up the mountainside in a wide single file, wary of an ambush and watching for sizzling sticks of dynamite. To his relief, the gang made decent time in spite of the treacherous footing. They skipped lunch and passed the spot where JT was hiding.

JT smiled as he noticed how spread out the gang was. He raised his spyglass, noticing a straggler bringing up the rear. The man was far behind the next closest outlaw. JT sat back, making no noise as the gang rode past and up the mountain. He watched as the second-to-last outlaw disappeared, then pulled out his Winchester and waited for the straggler.

Tim Yates was in charge of the two packhorses that carried the gang's food and supplies. In spite of that, he was seriously thinking of simply turning around and heading home. He reached for his canteen and was taking a swig when a quiet voice from behind him said, "Don't move or I'll blow you out of that saddle." He held the canteen and his other arm over his head, signifying his surrender. "Don't shoot, mister," he said over his shoulder.

JT moved closer. "Drop that canteen, shuck the Winchester out of the scabbard, and drop the Colt, NOW," JT said. "Then slide out of that saddle on this side, lie face down, and put your hands behind your back." Tim did exactly as he was told, shaking with fear.

JT pulled a short leather lariat out of his pocket, bound the man's wrists, then stuffed his bandana into his mouth. "You stay right there," JT ordered, as he returned to his hiding spot and gathered his belongings. He moved to a packhorse and threw his gear over its saddlebags. Then he tied his remaining Winchester and his bedroll to the saddle on the other packhorse and mounted Tim's horse.

"Okay, get up and head back down the mountain. We are going to have a little talk, just you and me. And if I don't like your answers, I'll skin you alive." Tim Yates nodded and tried to say something but the bandana prevented it.

As dusk settled in Duvall held up his hand. "Let's make camp here," he said. "I'm sure we are right behind him, so let's post guards overnight and get back at it in the morning."

One of the men called out, "Where is Yates? He's got the packhorses." He dismounted and climbed atop a boulder to see if he was still coming up the mountain. "Don't see him," he said. "Think he just up and left?"

Duvall thought a moment and said, "Well, if he did, that's more bounty for us."

The gang was not happy as they made camp. One man threw his gear to the ground, grumbling. "What good's money if we starve before we get it? Those horses had all our food!" The others nodded.

≈ ≈ ≈ ≈ ≈

JT and his prisoner headed slowly down the mountain. Tim was clinging to a packhorse's mane with his wrists tied in front of him, nearly falling off a couple of times. As they stopped just before dusk, JT unbound Tim and took the soaked bandanna out of his mouth. "Take care of the horses, then dig a hole," he said. Tim looked alarmed. "Don't worry; just deep enough to hide the campfire you're going to make," JT chuckled.

After a good dinner using the outlaws' supplies, JT pulled out the Scotch and poured it into his coffee cup. Tim looked up. "Ah, could I have some of that? It sure looks tasty."

JT snorted. "Why would I do that when I'm going to skin you?"

Tim hung his head. "No, please! I'll tell you whatever you want to know."

JT smiled and handed over the bottle. Tim started to chug it, and JT grabbed it back. "Whoa, take it easy!"

Tim hung his head. JT stared at him for a minute. "You look like a nice young fellow, so how did you get hooked up with these outlaws?" he asked.

"Well, that's a good question. When I met them, their leader was Sheriff Perez and the rest of them were deputies. I was at loose ends and I thought being a deputy was a good prospect. It wasn't until later that I figured out that they were really outlaws, but by then they wouldn't let me leave. I was doing their shit work, tending horses, cooking, waiting on them, taking their crap. Damn, they treated me like a slave! But then Sheriff Duvall showed up and started giving away more money than I'd ever seen. And of course, the $10,000 reward for you sounded pretty damn good. No offense."

JT chortled. "Yeah, how's that going for you so far?"

Tim stared at his boots. "Not so well, I guess."

"Okay, maybe I won't skin you," JT said with a smirk. "Tell me what the gang's attitude is. I know I've made a dent in the ranks, so what's their thinking?"

"You're not going to kill me?"

JT laughed. "Maybe or maybe not. What's your answer?"

"When you killed Sheriff Perez, that took the steam out of lots of the men. They had been riding with him for a long time. Then that darn dynamite scared the hell out of them. And the way you killed Arie in that damn pit, that was nasty!"

"Hey, I don't play patty cake with assholes who are trying to kill me. So, what else?"

"Well, Duvall pretty much took over after Perez was killed and began giving out money like it was water."

"That makes sense since it's not his money. It belongs to a jerk named Marcus Payne."

"Yeah, I heard Duvall and Perez talking about him." Tim looked over at the bottle of whiskey. "Could I have another drink, please?"

JT poured two fingers of Scotch into his coffee cup and handed it over. "Sip it, don't guzzle it. This isn't rotgut!"

Tim nodded. "Yes, sir. You're the boss!"

They sat quietly as JT pondered. *This young man seems to be a nice fellow; he may have simply gotten involved with the wrong crowd. And now he's calling me the boss? Could be good to have him on my side, if I can trust him.*

Chapter Twenty-One

Gregor put some of the gold in his saddlebags and, with a satisfied smiled on his face, headed back to Point Stevens Pass. He hadn't found JT, but the trip had certainly been rewarding, and he was looking forward to reuniting with Emma. He needed her womanly affection and good cooking, in that order.

He wondered how his new agents were doing with the posters. Gregor knew that the task was almost impossible, as he had no idea how many posters had been put up, but it was worth doing. Besides, they might stumble across a wanted man or two, and had been authorized to 'do what's right.'

JT wanted more than one man on the town-jumping task. Will Benjamin and Steffon Newman—two of Gregor's best men—had volunteered.

Will was a young, stocky, brown-haired man who could shoot the tail off a running jackrabbit at 200 feet. With a knife, this man was also the best Gregor had ever seen. He carried his Bowie knife in a scabbard on his gun belt, along with two smaller throwing knives. One was sheathed on his left side and one was hidden between his shoulder blades.

Gregor had seen his skills during his brief stint as a Pinkerton. One day, the four of them were between assignments, flush with money after catching three murderous bank robbers. They decided to take an early lunch at the local saloon. Will was having what he called a barley sandwich for lunch—a warm draft beer.

While the others played darts, Will watched with interest. After three games and no bulls-eyes, he spoke up. "I bet you I can hit the little red circle, first time," he said, taking out a twenty-dollar gold coin and setting it on the bar.

Gregor cocked his head. "So, you're matching all three of us?" Will smiled and nodded. Everyone grinned and anted up, slapping their coins on the bar.

"Can I get in on this?" the bartender inquired, as he placed a twenty on the bar. Will finished his beer and chuckled. "Why not? But if I win, you have to buy everyone in the place a drink!"

The bartender smiled. "You got a deal!" He'd seen that Will wasn't even warmed up and thought he had a safe bet.

Will stood at the mark on the saloon floor. Gregor started to hand a dart to him, but Will shook his head and simply stared ahead. The Pinks and the bartender glanced at each other with quizzical looks on their faces.

In a flash, Will reached to his left hip and threw a small knife at the dartboard. He smiled as he turned away and motioned toward the bartender. "Hey barkeep, how about those drinks?" he said, picking up the money from the bar.

Gregor stared at the dartboard with his mouth open. The knife was smack dab in the red bullseye.

The bartender looked at Will. "How the hell did you do that?"

Will smiled. "Get me my beer and I'll tell you."

The bartender set Will's beer down in front of him. "Okay, so?"

Will took a long drink of his beer, turned back to the dartboard, and in a heartbeat threw a second small knife from behind his shoulder blades. He smiled as it landed right next to the first, all but obliterating the red in the bullseye. He turned back to the astounded bartender and smiled. "Practice, my man—lots and lots of practice!"

The bartender laughed. "Drinks all around!" he yelled, as everyone cheered.

$$\approx \approx \approx \approx \approx$$

Duvall finally realized that Tim Yates was not coming back and that he had the packhorses with all the food supplies. The men knew it too and were cussing and swearing. Two of the men had bottles of rotgut in their saddlebags, which they passed around in lieu of supper.

Duvall strode up to the campfire from the surrounding darkness. "Okay, in the morning let's see if we can hunt down an elk or a mountain goat. I'll pay fifty dollars to the man who brings us one, and twenty dollars to anyone who makes the effort. In the meantime, finish those bottles and try to get a good night's sleep!"

A successful morning hunt netted three mountain goats, all from the same herd. Duvall called the men around the fire and handed out the promised money.

"We'll stay here for the day, butcher and smoke these animals and make jerky," he said. "Gus and Augie, you need to head down the mountain and see if you can catch up to our little traitor Yates. Don't shoot him unless you have to. Bring him back here and I'll deal with him."

He looked up the hillside. "Tomorrow we'll split into three groups and spread out on the mountain. If anyone spots Mr. JT Thomas, fire off three shots and the rest of us will come running." Duvall looked up at the cloudy sky. "Let's set up some lean-tos that we can build a fire under. Looks like it going to rain."

≈ ≈ ≈ ≈ ≈

In the morning, JT had made up his mind. "Mr. Yates, tell you what I'm going to do. I am not going to skin you after all. You seem like a nice fellow and I'm going to let you go, but you need to do something for me," he said.

Tim grinned. "Yes, whatever you say."

JT handed Tim a folded note. "Give this to my partner, Gregor Nelson, in Point Stevens Pass. Do you know where that is?"

Tim smiled. "Oh, you bet. My sister lives there."

"That's good, I hope," JT responded. "The note explains what is going on out here, and it tells him to hire you on. I left out the part about you running with Duvall and his gang, so don't make me regret this!"

"Why, thank you! I won't let you down! You sure are a good egg, Mr. JT."

JT cringed. "Well, let's get you started."

Just then, he heard a horse whinny nearby. "You stay here. I'm going to get the drop on whoever that is," he said, and quickly vanished into the forest.

Tim looked up as two horses rounded the bend. He held his hands in the air as the two outlaws rode straight for him, six-guns drawn.

"Well, well, well, Timmy boy," Augie snickered. "What do we have here?"

"Ah, I was j-just heading your way. I, uh, got lost in the dark last night," Tim stammered.

Gus laughed. "Don't bullshit an old bullshitter. You were lighting out. We might have let you go, but you got all our supplies! I'd like to shoot you right here, but Money Bags Duvall says to bring you back so he can do it himself."

JT emerged from the woods, just behind the men. "Turn around, fellows, and prepare to meet your maker," he said quietly.

Augie whipped his horse around, living just long enough to see JT with his Winchester at his shoulder before he got a hole through the chest.

Panting with fear, Gus drew his Colt and turned to face JT. "Sorry, too late," JT said, as he pumped two shots into his heart. As the man's body fell from the saddle, his horse turned and bolted back up the mountain.

Tim Yates stood with his hands still raised and his eyes closed. "Ah, Tim, you can open your eyes and lower your hands," JT said with a chuckle.

Tim did neither one, so JT spoke louder. "HEY TIM, YOU CAN LOWER YOUR HANDS AND OPEN YOUR EYES!"

Tim popped one eye open and slowly lowered his shaking hands. "Huh," was all he could manage to say.

JT laughed. "Come on, let's get going. Those fifty-caliber shots can be heard all the way to California."

They quickly packed up, with JT taking the packhorses and the gang's supplies. Tim tucked JT's note into his shirt pocket and mounted Augie's horse.

"Remember, find Gregor Nelson. He should be at the hotel," JT said.

Tim turned his horse and headed out, calling over his shoulder, "Take care, boss. Give 'em hell!"

Chapter Twenty-Two

As Gregor rode up to Buck's Livery, Buck stepped out of the back with a horseshoe in his hand.

"Well, look who is back!" Buck bellowed.

"Hello, Buck. How's my favorite stable owner?" Gregor said with a chuckle.

"Well, I'm fair to middlin'. Surely can't complain. Come on in and I'll tend to your horse as soon as I finish this," he said, holding up the horseshoe. He walked over to a tethered mare and lifted its hoof. Taking nails from his mouth, he quickly hammered on the new shoe, then smiled with satisfaction.

Gregor sat wearily on a bench. "So tell me, what's been going on since I left?"

"Not much, and that's a good thing. A couple more old Pinks stopped here," Buck said, pointing out an Appaloosa and a gelding. "They joined your buddies in guarding the town. Emma is getting ready to move out of the hotel and open her boarding house. Doc DeWitt and Dawn are busy planning their wedding, and I ain't seen hide nor hair of JT. I'm worried about him!" he said with a frown.

Gregor nodded. "Me too. I know he can take care of himself, but I wish I knew where he is at least."

Buck looked over at Gregor, whose stomach was growling. "Hey, you look dead on your feet and it sounds like you haven't eaten in a week. Go find the darlin' Emma and get some grub in ya!"

Gregor slapped Buck on the back. "Sounds good to me."

$$\approx \approx \approx \approx \approx$$

Duvall and his gang spent the day trying to stay out of the rain while roasting jerky over the fires. The men stuffed themselves with goat, whining about not having any coffee or whiskey. They were sitting miserably under their lean-tos when they heard a gunshot, and then another.

"Damn, that was loud!" one outlaw exclaimed. The man sitting next to him said, "Sounds like a fifty-caliber, and Gus and Augie don't have no fifty-caliber! Hell, neither does that goddamn Yates."

Duvall paused. *Hmmm, I bet I know who does.*

In the morning, it was still raining. Duvall and the men finished the roast goat, then divided the jerky between themselves and split up into three groups. "All right, you all have your instructions," Duvall said. "Saddle up and let's get this over with."

The men headed up the mountain, spreading out. Duvall had handpicked his group, knowing it was the most experienced and the most determined. They headed west and were soon out of sight of the others.

≈ ≈ ≈ ≈ ≈

JT put on his rain slicker and broke camp. He headed up the mountain toward the east slope, leading the packhorses through the steadily increasing rain.

As he made his way up the mountain, he thought about his friends in Point Stevens Pass, his beloved Annabelle, and his new detective agency. He laughed when he thought about the cougar. They didn't have cougars in Wisconsin where he grew up. *Are cougars red? Damned if I know.*

He was making good time despite the rain but decided he could do better if he went down to one packhorse. He stopped and went through the saddlebags, pulling out the supplies that he could leave behind and hiding them in a tiny cave behind a boulder. He slapped the unburdened packhorse on the butt and sent him off down the mountain, then continued up the slope.

≈ ≈ ≈ ≈ ≈

Lazlo Penn stopped near a stream on the mountainside, ahead of his outlaw friends. He was totally exhausted. He and his cohorts had abandoned their horses over two hours ago when the mounts simply couldn't keep going on the steep mountainside. One by one the rest of his associates had dropped off exhausted, grousing and cussing, but Lazlo was going to catch this damn JT Thomas or die trying.

Lazlo had grown up in Pennsylvania, with great parents, a stuck-up sister, and no prospects. In his early teens, his face broke out in small sores but, try as he may, he couldn't get them to go away. His mother, rest her soul, had tried to help, taking him to a doctor in spite of having no money. The doctor gave his mom an "ointment," whatever the hell that was. He said Lazlo had acne, which was common for an adolescent, and that it would go away in time. But it had not. It kept coming and coming, and now his face was filled with scars and pockmarks, dozens and dozens of them. It was a bitter pill; he had been a good-looking kid. His mother used to say he was even more handsome than his dad, and he was going to break a lot of hearts.

Lazlo heard a noise and his eyes popped open. He squinted and wiped his face with a wet sleeve. *I'll be damned, that's JT Thomas in the flesh! There must be a God, and He is smiling at me!*

He raised his Winchester to his shoulder, trying to take aim, but the end of the gun was moving back and forth. "Steady," he whispered to himself. He lowered it and wiped his face again. Taking a deep breath, he raised the gun, aimed it at JT's chest, and slowly pulled the trigger. He watched as JT spun and fell into the stream.

Chapter Twenty-Three

Back at the hotel, Gregor cleaned up and stowed his belongings, then walked over and knocked on Emma's door. The new receptionist stuck her head around the corner. "She is over at the boarding house. They are moving in the furniture from the warehouse," she said with a smile.

Gregor nodded and tipped his hat. Walking swiftly toward the newly rebuilt boarding house, he waved at the agent stationed on the rooftop. Emma was standing outside the yellow and blue structure, directing furniture traffic. "Looking good," Gregor said, as he approached her from behind.

Emma spun around, gave him a hug, and kissed him on the cheek. "It is going well. It was so nice of JT to give me these pieces. Some of them are worth a lot of money!" she said.

"Well, you know JT—generous to a fault. I just wish I knew where he was so I could help him!"

"Well, you might be in luck. Tim Yates rode into town late yesterday with a letter from JT. I just saw him at his sister's house on Maple Street."

"Who is Tim Yates?"

Emma paused as two movers stopped in front of her with the Crown Jewel desk. "That goes into JT's room. Top of the stairway and end of the hall, facing the street. Be careful with it!"

She turned back to Gregor. "Tim is a nice guy. A bit of a lost soul, but really sweet, and his sister Sarah is a good woman. She is married to Philip Bester, who runs the tonsorial parlor." She looked at Gregor's shaggy hair. "Maybe you should stop in there, introduce yourself, and get a haircut too!"

Gregor chuckled. "Maybe, but first I need to see that letter. Afterward, let's get an early dinner at the hotel. Or are you cooking there tonight?"

Emma smiled. "No, with the boarding house opening I gave my notice. So, I'll see you at four. We should be done here by then." She gave Gregor another peck on the cheek and he headed toward Maple Street.

Gregor found the Bester's place and knocked on the door. Tim's sister came to the door, holding a baby in her arms. "Well hello, Mr. Nelson. How are you today?" she asked.

"I'm fine. Have we met before?" Gregor replied.

"No, I don't think so, but we have been expecting you. Please come in. Would you like a cup of coffee? I just took cinnamon rolls out of the oven too, if you'd like one."

Gregor smiled and nodded as his stomach growled. "That would be wonderful!" he said.

"Oh my, perhaps you need two!" she said with a laugh. "Follow me. Tim's in here."

She led him into the kitchen, where Tim Yates was sitting at the table. Tim stood, introduced himself, and shook Gregor's hand. "I have a note for you from JT Thomas," he said.

As Gregor silently read the note, Sarah stood, pouring his cup of coffee with her right hand and holding the baby with her left. Tim stood up. "Can I hold the baby for you?" he asked.

Sarah smiled and handed the baby to Tim. "Why don't you put Lester in the cradle? It's his nap time." Tim smiled broadly and tiptoed out of the kitchen.

Gregor finished reading JT's letter, folded it, and put it in his shirt pocket as Sarah put two huge cinnamon rolls in front of him with a plate of softened butter.

"More coffee?" Sarah asked with a smile.

Gregor nodded as he lathered a cinnamon roll with butter. "Yes ma'am, that would be very nice!" He bit into the roll and groaned with a starving man's delight.

Gregor sipped his coffee as Tim returned and Sarah excused herself. "Tim, thanks for delivering the letter. JT says you're a good guy, and I'll take his word for it. Now tell me, could you find the place where you left JT?"

Tim nodded. "Sure I can, not a problem," he said, as he stuffed a huge piece of cinnamon roll in his mouth.

"Excellent. When can you leave?"

"Whenever you want, Mr. Nelson. Can I finish eating first?"

Gregor chuckled and stood up. "Go ahead. I'll be back tomorrow."

Chapter Twenty-Four

JT flew backward into the swift-flowing mountain stream. His eyes opened wide as he felt the icy water turn him around and around, out of control and struggling mightily to keep his head above water. The banks were steep and the water was nearly three feet deep, moving too quickly for him to get any kind of foothold. He desperately reached for a large pine branch that was racing downstream, but was spun around again, then smashed his head on a boulder and blacked out.

When he woke up, he was partially out of the water, caught on a snag of branches. He lay there unmoving. *Am I dead?* he wondered briefly. But the intense pain and biting cold told him otherwise.

JT felt a tug on his battered coat collar as he was pulled out of the river and up onto the bank. He felt the sun on his back as he opened his eyes, his teeth chattering and his head feeling woozy. He rolled over and tried to sit up, but immediately turned his head and retched river water. He knew if he didn't get up soon he would be dead from exposure, to say nothing of the gunshot.

Slowly he sat up and looked around. There was no one near him, and even in his fuzzy condition he wondered how he had come to rest on a sunny flat boulder. He looked down at his coat and his pants. They were ruined and soaking wet. Slowly and painfully, he removed his coat, shirt, pants, and long johns. He looked at his boots and sighed. It was too much—he couldn't possibly take them off.

Naked and freezing, he lay down and made peace with his God.

≈≈≈≈≈

Will Benjamin and Stiff Diggs stood in the Dry Bluff Saloon in the small town of Starkvale, Colorado, drinking beer and taking advantage of the free cheese and pickled eggs the bartender had offered them. At a table were three old men who looked like they had been there since breakfast, laughing and playing poker for peanut shells. Another man sat in the far corner, sipping rotgut with his Stetson pulled down over his face. Two ranch cowboys at the far end of the bar also were enjoying beer and the free meal.

Will pointed at the poster of JT on the wall. "Well, there is another one. I wonder who put them up?" he said, glancing at the bartender.

"That was some sheriff that I'd never seen before," the bartender said. "I think he said his name was Duvall. Didn't seem like a nice guy, if you get my drift. Paid for a good whiskey, ate the cheese and eggs, and left a nice tip. But you could see in his eyes that he would shoot you in a heartbeat if he wanted to. He put the poster up without asking and told me that if I took it down there would be hell to pay. I damn near tore it down, but…"

Will nodded that he understood. He pulled out JT's replacement poster and handed it to Stiff. "You want to do the honors?"

Stiff chuckled and finished his beer. He grabbed the new poster and moseyed over, chewing a chunk of cheese. He pulled the poster down and began putting the new one up, using the handle of his pistol to pound in the small nails.

The man seated at the table looked up from his whiskey and pushed his hat back on his head. "What the hell are you doing?" he demanded.

Stiff finished nailing the poster in place and turned around. "Well, my friend, you can have a look for yourself. That old poster isn't good any more, and this new one says that Mr. John Thurgood Thomas is exonerated and no reward will be paid. It's signed by the Governor of Missouri. So, there you have it."

The man threw back his whiskey and stood up. "I don't believe you. I was just fixin' to chase this JT Thomas and I ain't about to give up $10,000 on your say-so. I think you're lying and you just want the reward for yourself!"

Stiff looked over at Will, who was watching with amusement while eating a pickled egg. Will shrugged and nodded, indicating Stiff should have at it. Stiff moved his hand near his Smith and Wesson Model 3 revolver. "Did you just call me a liar?" he asked, his eyes burning a hole through the man.

"You bet I did, and I think you're a damn coward as well," the man replied.

Stiff looked over at Will. "Did you hear that?"

Will tossed a small piece of cheese in the air and caught it in his mouth. "Yep."

Stiff shook his head. "What's your name, mister?" he said quietly.

"My name is Chet Gibson, and I'm going to gut shoot you and watch you die slowly."

Stiff looked at the man but spoke to Will. "Hey Will, did you hear that? This is the notorious Chet Gibson! Bank robber, murderer, and rapist. Why, I do believe he is wanted dead or alive for $1,000."

Gibson bared his teeth and replied, "Yeah, that's me, but you ain't going to be collecting any reward. I'm going to kill you and your cheese-eating friend," he said, as he and Stiff went for their guns.

Gibson's Colt was half out of his holster when a knife hit him right in the heart. Stiff turned and looked at Will. "Hey, he said he was going to kill me too," Will said, and took a sip of his beer.

Stiff holstered his pistol, shook his head, and moved back to the bar, where he took Will's beer and guzzled it. "Okay by me, but we are going to share the reward."

Will smiled and called for another round. "Wouldn't have it any other way," he said with a snort.

≈ ≈ ≈ ≈ ≈

Peering into the raging river, Lazlo Penn fired three quick shots into the air to summon his outlaw buddies. He shook his head. JT was nowhere in sight. *No JT means no reward.*

Two men emerged from the rainy mist. "What's up?" the first man inquired.

"I... ah... found him," Lazlo replied, just as Duvall and three others joined them.

"I heard that," Duvall said. "So, where is he?"

Lazlo pointed at the frigid stream. "I hit him, but he went ass over tea kettle into the river," he said, pointing downstream.

"Son of a bitch," Duvall said. "Son of a BITCH!"

One of Duvall's companions pointed at a horse standing twenty yards away, calmly munching on grass. "Hey, ain't that one of our pack horses?"

The outlaw reached over and undid the strap on the saddlebags. He reached inside, pulled out a can of beans, and held it above his head. Duvall smiled, pulled his Colt out of his holster, and fired three shots into the air, signaling the other group. Looking up at the sky, he said, "Going to be dark soon, so let's make camp here and go find that damn JT Thomas in the morning. He fell in the water, so my guess is he's somewhere downstream. He can't be far, anyway."

The men dismounted and began to make camp, smiling and slapping each other's backs. The cook unloaded the packhorses and held up half a bottle of Scotch whiskey. "Looky here, see what I found!" he said, dancing a little jig.

Duvall chuckled. "Let's get settled and get some food in our stomachs before we down that!"

As the cook dished out supper, the rest of the outlaws finally appeared and dismounted, grumbling that Tim Yates wasn't there to take care of their horses. But when the cook filled their plates with the recovered food, the grumbling turned into grins. "Just in time. I never want to eat another goat!" one man laughed.

After everyone was done eating, Duvall took the whiskey and divided it up as best he could, then held his tin cup in the air for a toast.

"Here's to capturing JT Thomas—or at least his corpse—in the morning," he said, as he clinked cups with the man seated next to him.

"Hear, hear," the gang yelled.

Chapter Twenty-Five

In JT's dream, he was freezing cold and his ears were being bombarded with growls, growls, and more growls. He snapped awake and rolled over, attempting to sit up. In front of him on the rock slab was the red cougar, snarling and growling intermittently. Around them was a small pack of wolves, nearly drowning out the cougar with their own growls.

As JT began to stand up, the cat crouched low and leaped at the largest wolf, raking it across the eyes. She struck once, twice, three times in the blink of an eye. The wolf let out a scream and began pawing at his bloody face. The cougar looked over her shoulder at JT, as if she were wondering why he was still there, then hurled herself at the rest of the pack.

JT tried to get at his torn-up clothes, but nearly fainted when he stood up too fast. He took one more look at his guardian angel that seemed to be in the fight of her life. Then he shook his woozy head, gingerly jumped down from the rock, and ran into the forest, naked but for his boots and socks.

He ran, tripping over dead branches but jumping back up and continuing on until he was out of breath. He sat on a log and realized two things: he wasn't feeling any pain or cold, and he had no idea where he was.

JT looked around in the gathering dusk. Red, brown, orange, and yellow leaves covered the forest floor, with a few green ones mixed in. He had no idea how far he had run, but he certainly did not hear the snarls and growls of the fighting animals. He gingerly rubbed his head, still woozy from the blow he had received.

He made himself a cushion of leaves and collapsed into it. As he lay looking at the darkening sky, the cold began to return. He burrowed as best he could into the pile and wrapped his arms over his chest. As he drifted off with teeth chattering and wondering if this was the end for him, he heard the tinkling of a sleigh bell in the distance.

$$\approx \approx \approx \approx \approx$$

Duvall's gang resumed the hunt for JT the next morning. Before long, they reached the rock where JT's clothing was drying in the sun. One of the outlaws reached over and picked up the long johns with a stick. "Hey Devon," he said to his sidekick, "these look to be in pretty good shape. Why don't you throw your crappy ones away?" The men laughed and Devon gave a toothy grin.

Duvall crossed the stream and rode up to the two men. He looked at the clothing on the rock and started to laugh. "My God!" he exclaimed, "old JT Thomas looks to be naked as a jaybird! Oh, this is sweet—he's unarmed and probably frozen to death. Let's spread out men, and look for lumps in the leaves!"

In high spirits, the men began the search again in earnest.

≈ ≈ ≈ ≈ ≈

Gregor met Emma at the hotel café at four as planned. "Well, how did it go with the furniture move?" Gregor inquired.

"We finished up a half hour ago and it sure looks nice. The cave furniture really complements the new pieces I purchased. Thank God for JT Thomas and his generosity! I'm going to pay him back all the money he advanced me before he left," she said, then turned serious. "Do you think he's okay?"

"Oh, I'm sure he is fine. Probably making himself supper right now over a campfire. He's an adventurous sort, so he's probably enjoying the chase."

Emma nodded skeptically.

"Actually, I had quite an adventure myself," Gregor said, and proceeded to tell Emma about the cave, Jean, the dynamite, and the gold.

"Gregor, you could have been killed!" Emma exclaimed, reaching out and taking his hand.

He smiled into her eyes. "Don't worry, I've had a lot of practice in not getting killed, and luck is on my side. But talk about luck—JT seems to be getting richer on a weekly basis!"

"What are you going to do?" Emma asked.

"Well, I'm going to contact my mining experts in Golden. I want them to bring their crew and set up a mining operation as soon as possible. In the meantime, I'll send a few of the ex-Pinks to guard the cave."

Emma nodded. "That's a good idea. I just wish we could help JT!"

JT woke from a dream where he was snuggled up to something warm and furry. He opened his eyes and looked around. His boots and his head were cold, but the rest of him wasn't. As he stood up, he heard a noise in the forest and saw a flash of red. *Looks like my guardian angel is still around!*

JT knew he was lost, but he gauged the sun's direction and headed south. He was beginning to feel the cold again, but his head felt much better and his wound seemed to be okay as well. He felt it front and back and nodded with satisfaction.

Through and through—that's good. And most of the blood is gone. Licked off, maybe?

He felt well enough for a slow run, enough to at least warm him up a bit. As the day wore on, he stopped when he was out of breath and picked up again when the cold settled into his bones.

It was late afternoon when he broke out of the trees into a wide clearing. In the middle was a burned farmhouse and a large number of intact chicken coops. On the other side of the expanse was a building that also was untouched by the fire. JT walked toward it, passing a few chickens and a rooster as snowflakes began to fall around him. His teeth were chattering from the cold, and he was glad for the chance to get out of the snow. The building appeared to be unoccupied, with a large, crude sign above the door that said *EGGS, CHICKENS AND PILLOWS.*

The door was unlocked, so he entered the building. The front of the building appeared to be an office, about thirty by fifteen feet, with a large desk and a wood-burning stove in the corner and two doors on the back wall. JT moved quickly to the one on the left. It was a utility closet, with a broom, mop, and bucket. There were also assorted tools inside, and a full-length mirror on the back of the door.

JT moved to the other door, opened it, and stepped into a loading space. There were windows and barn doors that led out to the side yard on one wall, and he saw another door on the opposite side. He walked over to it, stepped through, and stopped in amazement.

The room was full of pillows! Pillows from top to bottom and side to side. JT nearly laughed, bending down to pick up a few feathers. He reached out and grabbed a feather pillow and held it to his chest. It was cold, but not as cold as he was.

JT left the door behind him open, letting in some light, and smiled as he burrowed into the nearest stack until pillows surrounded him. He rearranged a few pillows above his head, giving himself a space to breathe. Very slowly, he began to feel a little warmer. He sighed to himself, now realizing how exhausted he was from the run through the forest. He slowly drifted off, thinking about the cougar.

Red, my guardian angel.

Chapter Twenty-Six

Will Benjamin and Stiff Diggs dropped the wanted man off at the sheriff's office and headed for the nearest boarding house. The sheriff let them know that the bank was closed, so they wouldn't be paid until the next day. They both smiled and nodded, thinking they could use a long night's sleep in a comfy bed.

The next morning, they were just finishing their breakfast at the café when the sheriff stuck his head in the door. "I'm heading to the bank to get your money. I'll be back in a bit," he said.

Stiff signaled to the waitress. "Ma'am, could you warm this up?" he asked, as he handed the coffee pot to the young woman.

"Ma'am? Do I look like some old lady?" she asked with a scowl.

Will chuckled. "Not at all. In fact, you're a mighty pretty young lady. Don't mind my friend Stiff here."

The waitress smiled at Will. "Well, thank you kindly." She turned to Stiff. "What kind of name is Stiff? It sounds like the name of a dead man."

Stiff looked up defiantly. "Well, I'm told that when I'm in a gunfight I stand straight and tall, and look like I'm stiff."

The waitress shook her head as she turned toward the kitchen. "That's the dumbest thing I have ever heard."

Will laughed and Stiff shrugged his shoulders. "Didn't mean no offense," he said.

They were waiting for their fresh coffee when they heard gunshots coming from the bank. Will quickly stood up, throwing money on the table and picking up his hat. Stiff jumped up and followed him out the door with his Smith and Wesson Model 3 in his hand.

They hurried toward the bank to find the sheriff collapsed on the bank steps, holding his stomach. Three men emerged from the bank with bandanas over their faces, each holding a bag in their left fist and a Colt revolver in their right. The lead robber spotted Will, raised his six-gun, and let off a wild shot that landed in front of Will. Will returned the favor and ducked into a storefront.

The robbers quickly mounted their horses and galloped out of town. Stiff fanned his revolver at them, but he knew they were already out of range. Will and Stiff hurried over to the sheriff, who was holding his stomach and grimacing in pain.

"Ah, goddamn," the sheriff said. "I'm gut shot!"

Will looked at the dying man. "I'm sorry, Sheriff, but you best make peace with your Maker."

The sheriff nodded. "I'll do that," he said, then whispered a prayer and died.

Stiff looked at Will. "Well, this is personal now. They got away with our reward money!"

Xavier Duvall led his gang of happy outlaws through the mountain forest as the rain began to change to fluffy snow. The afternoon sun had begun to set when he heard snarling off to his right. He stopped his horse and headed toward the sound. He wove around pine trees and leafless deciduous trees, getting closer to the noise. Emerging into an open grassy spot, he spotted the largest cougar he had ever seen standing over one of his men. The red cat had its jaws wrapped around the man's neck and was shaking him back and forth. The outlaw was screaming and batting at the cat, to no avail. Suddenly, the cougar gave one last shake and the screaming stopped.

Duvall, frozen in his saddle, did not even attempt to raise his gun. The cougar, her lips a bloody red, looked at him. He could have sworn she was smiling. The cat stood quietly, placed her paw on the dead man's chest and pressed down on his heart, then turned and bounded into the forest. Duvall heard something strange: the sound of sleigh bells.

JT woke up disoriented but toasty warm, except for his wet boots. It took a moment before he realized where he was. He stretched and smiled, then rolled toward the small bit of light he could see through the open door. Standing up, he headed to the loading dock, spitting a feather out of his mouth. As he peeked through a crack in the outer doors, he saw the snow was coming down heavier now.

JT hurried to the stove in the office and was delighted to see a book of matches sitting on top. He opened the stove and smiled. Wood and kindling were stacked neatly inside, which he quickly lit. He looked around, hoping to spot some additional wood, but was disappointed. He went to the utility closet, grabbed the mop, and tried unsuccessfully to snap the handle over his thigh.

Next, he went to the desk, pulled out the top drawer, and unceremoniously dumped the contents on top. Deciding not to try breaking the drawer over his leg, he went back into the utility closet and grabbed the hammer. He returned and smashed the drawer to pieces with a smile on his face and an aching thigh. He stuffed the broken pieces into the stove as his teeth began to chatter again. When he pulled out the rest of the drawers, he was happy to find two full bags of coffee in one of them. JT then took the hammer to the drawers until he had a small pile of fuel for the fire.

The stove, while heating the corner of the room where it was situated, did little to heat the rest of the office. He pulled the desk chair over, sat down, and pulled off his wet boots and socks with a struggle. He put the boots on the seat of the chair and hung the socks off the back to dry. JT stood in the corner with his hands out to the rapidly-heating stove and assessed his situation. Suddenly, it dawned on him.

Feathers, pillows, cloth: warmth!

JT quickly spun around and headed back to the warehouse, grabbed as many pillows as he could, and returned to the office. Standing next to the stove, he grabbed a pillow by the bottom and pulled and pulled, trying to get the seam to separate. It did not.

Damn, pretty well-made pillows!

JT spotted the open door to the utility closet with the mirror hung on it. He grinned as he picked up the hammer, removed the mirror, and went to the far end of the room. He gently popped the mirror, which cracked but did not break. He hit the mirror harder and the cracks widened, so he reversed the hammer and used the claw end to gently lift a sharp piece of glass out of the frame.

He hurried back to the warm corner and picked up the pillow he had been working on. With the glass shard, he sliced the bottom of the pillow and feathers began to spill out. He cut more of the fabric and began to shake the pillow as the feathers flew around him. Then, he quickly made a slice in the top of the pillow, enough to put his head through, and two more on the sides for his arms. He laughed as he pulled his new shirt on over his head, then snatched the next pillow off the floor and repeated the process three more times.

JT fed more wood into the stove, then went back and grabbed another handful of pillows. As he returned to the office, he noticed scissors sitting on the desk. *Idiot!* he thought, slapping his head. Grabbing them, he moved back into the heated corner and began to cut open another pillow. He set to work making himself what could only be described as a diaper, and then made two more. Next came the pant legs. JT slipped pillowcases over his legs, tying them on with strips cut from another pillow. The morning melted away and the fire was nearly gone when JT finished, putting his dry socks back on and his nearly dry boots.

JT stood up and walked over to the remains of the mirror. He looked like a snowman—an abominable snowman at that. "But I'm a WARM abominable snowman!" he said to himself, laughing.

Chapter Twenty-Seven

Duvall and his gang kept up the search for JT until it began to get dark. The euphoria of the morning was gone, along with the whiskey and any warmth the daylight provided. They made camp, digging several fire pits so each man could bed down near the flames. They ate a quick dinner and went to bed early, which made Duvall happy since he didn't have to hear any more grousing.

In the morning he was up early, drinking coffee while the camp cook made bacon and flapjacks. As the gang came over with their plates and coffee cups, Duvall tried to provide some encouragement. "We will find JT Thomas today and get the hell off this mountainside," he said. Some men nodded; most had nothing to say.

They broke camp and resumed their careful scouting of the forest for JT, while the snow started to drift down through the canopy. Duvall was feeling wary.

God, I hope we find him today. These guys are getting antsy.

Will Benjamin and Stiff Diggs stood over the sheriff as the bank manager stepped down the stairs, holding on to his bloody shoulder. "Aw, no, is he dead?" he asked.

Will nodded. "Sure is. What happened here?"

"They killed my teller and winged me when I wouldn't open the safe fast enough!" the man exclaimed.

"How much did they take?" Stiff inquired.

"Over $40,000," the bank manager wailed.

"Hmm. So, would you like us to follow them and bring your money back?"

"Oh my, that would be wonderful!"

Will and Stiff crossed their arms across their chests and smiled at the banker expectantly. The banker looked confused and said, "Ah, I think they are getting away!"

Will looked at the road leading out of town. "Yep, I believe you are right."

The manager attempted a small smile. "Oh, you would like to perhaps get a reward?"

Stiff and Will smiled and nodded but remained silent.

"Uh, I'm not the owner. But since time is of the essence, I guess I could offer, say, $1,000."

Will looked at Stiff, then back at the banker. "How many bank robbers were there?"

"Three," he replied, fidgeting.

"So, $1,000 for each?"

The bank manager scuffed his boot toes into the dirt. "Aw, hell. Yes, $1,000 each. But get going!"

Will and Stiff uncrossed their arms, turned, and headed for their mounts.

≈ ≈ ≈ ≈ ≈

Following the tracks was easy since they were fresh and deep, indicating fast-moving horses. Stiff and Will stretched their horses into a gallop, riding until they were winded. They took a rest and Stiff looked over at Will, who was taking a swig out of his canteen. "Looks like they may be slowing down."

"Well, they haven't given their horses a break as far as I can see. If they don't slow down, someone's horse is gonna just up and collapse," Will replied, as he capped his canteen.

"Then let's get moving. I'd like to be there for that!" Stiff grinned.

The duo rode for another half hour when the outlaw's tracks split into three different directions. Stiff raised his hand and pulled up his horse. Will followed suit and slipped out of the saddle. He filled his hat from his canteen and offered it to his winded horse, then let Stiff's horse drink as well. "Hope we see a stream soon. I'm empty," Will said, as he climbed back into his saddle.

"Which way should we go now?" Stiff inquired.

Will pointed to the right. "Lamberton is about fifteen miles that way. They got no law, but they do have a saloon with pretty good grub. And some soiled doves," he grinned.

Stiff smiled. "Lead the way, partner. I'm hungry."

The two of them rode into Lamberton, avoiding the main street and circling around to the livery stable on the outskirts. They pulled out their Winchesters and rode quickly inside. A small young fellow was washing down a horse that looked as if it were about to collapse. Water from a large sponge ran down his arm as he raised his hands over his head. "I give up!" he squeaked.

Will smiled and placed his rifle back into its scabbard. "Sorry boy, but we are chasing a bank robber. We were hoping to get the drop on him."

The boy nodded and Will and Stiff dismounted. "Well, the man who just dropped off this horse had a bank bag slung over his horn. He stuffed it in his saddlebags and took it, along with a nice-looking Sharps rifle. He said something about getting a drink and some womanly comfort."

Stiff tossed the boy a five-dollar coin. "Clean them up and feed them oats, not hay. And if you've got an apple or two, they would appreciate it. We will be back in the morning."

Stiff and Will headed for the saloon. "I told you his horse would collapse!" Will said with a smile.

"Yep, it damn near did. Now keep an eye out in there. This bank robber probably doesn't know us, so let's keep it that way until we figure out who he is."

Will nodded and pushed through the swinging doors. One man was standing at the far end of the bar with a bottle of bourbon in front of him and a saddlebag at his feet. There was a group of locals playing poker at a corner table, laughing and tossing back whiskey.

Will and Stiff moved to the other end of the bar. "Hello, gents," the bartender said. "Never seen you before. Just passin' through?"

Stiff just nodded, but Will spoke up. "Oh, I've been here once or twice before, just not for a few years."

The barkeep grinned. "Well, I've been here for less than a year, but welcome back. My name is Mack, by the way."

"Hello Mack, pleased to make your acquaintance," Stiff said. "We would like a bite to eat. My partner Will says you have some mighty fine grub here."

"Oh, you bet we do. The owner and his wife do all the cooking, and they do a dandy job of it. They both used to be chefs in St. Louis, at least 'til the wife killed a banker. She got off scot-free though, 'cause no one likes a banker," he said with a smile. "And it must be your lucky day, because today we're serving the best fried chicken in Colorado. Plus, your first round of drinks is on that guy," he said, pointing at the man at the other end of the bar. "He says he just came across some easy money and wanted to share it!"

Just then a man with a satisfied smile came down the steps and headed out the door. A moment later a mature but still attractive woman made her way down the curving staircase. She made her way to the man at the end of the bar, picked up his whiskey glass, and downed it in a heartbeat. "Thanks for waiting for me. I'm ready if you are!"

The bank robber spoke quietly to the bartender, who went into the back room with a smile on his face. He returned with two bottles of bourbon and took a twenty-dollar bill in exchange.

The outlaw grinned at the woman and picked up his saddlebag. "Grab those bottles and lead the way, little lady, and get ready for a long night of ecstasy!"

Mack slid the bourbon over to Will and Stiff. "That man said you fellas should take this and have a good time, on him!"

Will smiled and Stiff did not as the kitchen door opened and the cook emerged. He reached up to set two big plates of steaming chicken, mashed potatoes, and corn on the bar. Will and Stiff looked down at the man, who appeared to be under five feet tall. The cook looked up at the six-foot-three Stiff and shook his head. "Don't let it get cold," he said, then turned on his heel and hurried back into the kitchen.

Will and Stiff chuckled as they dug into the tasty chicken. It was as good as Mack said it was. After the meal was done, Stiff filled their whiskey glasses and told Mack to come over and bring a glass for himself. Mack smiled as he set the glass down in front of Stiff, who filled it to the top.

"So, our bourbon-buying friend is staying the night?" Will asked.

Mack nodded. "Oh yes, he paid for Lettie for the night. Sounds like he is getting a lot of exercise and sleeping in, if you know what I mean."

"Do you have a couple more rooms available?"

"You bet, but if you want any companionship you will need to wait until the cook is done."

Stiff stared at the bartender. "Are you telling me the cook's wife is a soiled dove?"

Mack smiled as he refilled his glass and took a sip. "Not just her—both of them!"

Chapter Twenty-Eight

JT heard his stomach rumble as he looked up from the mirror. He sat down and put on his warm socks, wrapping a few strips of pillowcases around them for added warmth, then put on his nearly-dry boots and headed outside. Walking through snow flurries, he checked out the chicken coops. The first six were empty, but in the seventh he found the treasure he was looking for. A half-dozen chickens were sitting on eggs and a huge Plymouth Rock cockerel was perching in the rafters.

JT stepped into the shed and the rooster immediately swooped down at him. He quickly retreated into the ever-increasing snow as the rooster stopped at the entrance and made a loud "oh-oh" sound, designed to chase JT away.

He looked around for something to hit the rooster with. He thought about getting the broom handle but decided to search the burned-out farmhouse instead, hoping to find a cast iron skillet large enough to smack a protective rooster with and cook chicken and eggs in.

As he made his way through the debris, he stopped at the sight of two charred skeletons in what he assumed to be have been a bed. JT made the sign of the cross continued his hunt. In the back corner he found what he was looking for, along with an additional surprise. A few feet away from the group of cast iron skillets and pans he found a pile of assorted knives. The wooden handles were gone, but the blades and tangs were intact. JT smiled as he picked up a handful of knives, including a large butcher knife. He placed them in a large pan and then placed that in the cast iron skillet.

JT took his haul and moved past the chicken coop, stopping at the warehouse door. Pulling out the butcher's knife, he headed back toward the coop. The rooster lurched at JT, his spurs poised to slice JT's leg. JT, however, was ready, having dealt with roosters as a boy. He swung the knife and neatly sliced off the rooster's head. His body continued to run around the yard, even though he was now headless.

JT grabbed a hen and beheaded it. He killed another one, then gathered the eggs they had been sitting on and placed them gently into the pot. He picked up the carcasses by the feet and headed toward the warehouse, now nearly invisible in the heavy snow.

Inside, he grabbed the hammer and broke up the rest of the desk. He quickly fed the stove, his stomach growling all the while. After setting the eggs on the stove to boil, he went to work ripping the feathers off the chickens. He slit open and gutted them, then cut them apart at the joints. Using the fatty tails to grease the pan, he tossed the cut-up chicken into the hot skillet.

Fifteen minutes later, it was ready to eat. The meat was piping hot as he dug in. JT thought, *Oh my God, that is absolutely delicious!*

Duvall's gang had spread out and were nearly invisible to each other in the densely falling snow. Suddenly, there was a shot fired to his right and a voice yelled out, "I got him! I got him!"

Duvall rode up just as the shooter, a man named Pookie, rolled over the body, then looked up and groaned. The man looking over Pookie's shoulder slapped him on the back of his head, sending his hat into the snow. "You son of a bitch, you done gone and killed Chester, God damn you!" he shouted. Duvall moved up and confirmed that the dead man was in fact Chester, and not JT Thomas.

Pookie pleaded with Duvall. "Hey, he wasn't supposed to get out in front of us! And I couldn't see anything through this goddamned snow. It wasn't my fault! It was an honest mistake!"

Duvall quickly drew his Colt and put a slug in between Pookie's eyes. "Yep, just an honest mistake, you horse's ass!" he growled. Turning to the rest of the gang, he said, "Put up some lean-tos and build a fire. We might as well have an early meal since this snow don't look like it's about to end."

A somber man rode up to Duvall and pointed to the bodies. "Should we bury them?" he asked.

Duvall nodded. "Bury Chester but not Pookie. Leave him for the wolves and coyotes." The man smiled and went to get a shovel from the packhorse.

After a small meal, Duvall lay shivering in his bedroll, looking at the heavy snow and thinking dejectedly, *This whole thing is a mess, and now this snow is going to cover JT's tracks. We may never find him, damn it!*

≈ ≈ ≈ ≈ ≈

Will and Stiff woke up in the morning to the smell of coffee and bacon. Will knocked quietly on Stiff's door. Stiff was up and dressed already, and they tiptoed by the bank robber's door. Making their way down the long winding stairway, they sat at a table in the corner with a view of the stairs. Mack came out of the kitchen with a pot of coffee and two mugs. He set them in front of them and filled them up. "Good morning!" he said cheerfully.

"Has our bank robber been down yet?" Will inquired.

Mack chuckled. "No, he surely ain't. I'm guessing we won't see him till later if he and Lettie drank both of those bottles. The good news is we have hash, eggs, bacon, ham, and flapjacks with blueberries. Maple syrup and plenty of butter, too. The chefs got no takers last night, so they got up early to prepare a feast."

Will smiled. "That sounds good, and keep the coffee coming too!"

Mack nodded, setting the pot down on the table as the chef's wife came through the swinging doors with two plates loaded with eggs, hash, and bacon. She was followed by her short husband, who was carrying plates of blueberry flapjacks and ham. "You enjoy," the woman said. "Mack tells me you are chasing a bank robber. While I don't hold much stock in bankers, I don't believe in stealing either," she said.

Will smiled and began to dig in. Stiff stood up and nodded to her. "Thank you kindly. This looks too good to be true!"

The woman smiled and looked Stiff up and down. "Well, I sure wish I would have married you instead of this little shrimp," she said, pointing at her husband, then turned and headed back into the kitchen.

The little man grinned. "I don't take it personally. She says stuff like that when she's looking for johns."

"I understand. Ah, how tall is she, if you don't mind me asking?" Stiff inquired.

Her husband smiled. "Six foot two and then some," he said, as he headed back into the kitchen.

The saloon began to fill up, and nearly half the customers were women. The two-hour breakfast rush caused Mack to shut down the bar, since he was busy helping the cooks shuttle food out of the kitchen. Will and Stiff gave up their table and drank coffee at the bar.

As the place began to empty out, the bank robber made his way down the staircase with bloodshot eyes. He reeked of bourbon. He nodded at Will and Stiff, who had returned to their table. Mack sauntered over to him. "Good morning! How are you on this fine morning?" Mack bellowed.

The man hung his head. "Hey, can I get some breakfast? I'm mighty hungry."

Mack looked over at Will and Stiff. "Sorry, partner, breakfast was over some time ago. How about some coffee?"

The robber shuddered. "Not on an empty stomach. Give me a double shot of brandy, blackberry brandy if you have it, and a beer on the side."

Mack reached up on the shelf behind him and took down a dusty bottle of blackberry brandy. He poured two fingers in a glass, drew a warm beer, and set the glasses on the bar. "That's on the house, my friend. I'm thinking that may be the last drink you are ever going to have," he said quietly.

Stiff and Will stood up, pointing their six-guns at the robber. The man poured the brandy down his throat and threw the empty glass at Stiff, who dodged it with ease.

A door opened at the top of the stairs and an oblivious Lettie sashayed down the winding staircase, distracting Will and Stiff long enough for the robber to dash up the steps. "I'll kill her if you men make a move," he shouted. "Now holster those guns and we will walk out of here. Nobody needs to get hurt."

Will looked over at Stiff, who nodded his agreement. Both men holstered their weapons and Will moved closer to the staircase. Lettie and the bank robber were moving slowly down the steps when Will reached behind his neck and let his hidden knife fly, hitting the robber in the middle of his cheek. The man grabbed his face as Lettie stomped on his foot and ran down the stairs. The bank robber raised his six-gun and fired at Will, missing by a mile. Stiff raised his Smith & Wesson and fired one shot into the man's midsection. He immediately bent over, rolled down the stairs, and landed at the bottom with a thud. He fired a last shot, hitting Lettie in the face. She fell to the ground, writhing in excruciating pain.

Stiff knelt next to the fallen robber. "God, it hurts! Help me!" the man begged.

Stiff nodded. "Yes, I know. You are gut shot and it hurts like a bitch. I'm thinking you're going to die in, oh I don't know, a few hours."

"Oh my God," the man gasped. "Shoot me, please shoot me!" Stiff looked over at Will. Will shrugged, indicating it was Stiff's decision to make.

Stiff turned back to the groaning, whimpering robber with a quizzical look on his face. "Now why would I do that? Geez, that would be murder! And hell, you are going to die anyway."

"Oh please, please, I'll tell you where my partners are!"

Stiff actually smiled. "Okay, but if you're lying to me, I'll come back, dig up your grave, have you hanged in the public square, and let the fine citizens spit on your sorry dead self!"

The bank robber grimaced. "You wouldn't do that. That's just plain mean!"

Stiff smiled his evil smile again. "Oh, I would. I surely would."

The man nodded. "Okay, okay, I believe you, and this is the truth, I swear on my mother's grave. Cody Newton is headed to his brother's cabin in Ashcroft, and Snake Brill is headed to his mother's home in St. Elmo."

Will walked up to Stiff. "Lettie's gone," he said quietly.

Stiff nodded and pulled the man up close. "Guess what, your date from last night just died because of you. Oh, and I lied. You'll suffer, you asshole, and may you rot in hell!"

Mack moved up and kicked the man in his bleeding stomach. "Lettie was my sister, you bastard!" he growled. "You are going to die in agony. I'll make sure of that."

Chapter Twenty-Nine

JT had a plan. He stood up and went to the utility closet, grabbed the mop and two cans of kerosene. He left the fuel next to the warehouse doors and stuck the mop head onto the stove. Stepping outside, he made deliberate deep steps into the deep snow. He headed directly toward the forest, taking his time and making sure his footprints were deep and visible. Fifty yards in, he stopped, reversed himself and slowly retraced his steps backward until he was back at the doors. He repeated the drill in each direction, then retraced the trail to the east for good measure since he assumed that is where Duvall and his gang would be coming from. When he was done, he gathered his food and supplies into pillowcases and deliberately made his way up the mountain, dropping everything at the edge of the forest.

He returned to the warehouse and pulled the mop handle out of the stove. The mop was, as expected, burned up, but the rest of the handle was intact. JT sat down on the floor with a hammer, a pair of pliers, a pile of thin nails, some pillow strips, and a seven-inch knife.

He placed the knife on the end of the pole and bound it tightly with three strips of cloth, then carefully drove a nail through one of the holes in the tang and the wood. When it was halfway through the mop handle, he bent it over the pole with the pliers and tapped it snug with the hammer. He did the same through the remaining two holes, then wrapped the pole in the remaining pillow strips and tied them off. JT stood up and tapped his new spear on the warehouse floor, then took it outside and smiled as it easily pierced the frozen ground.

Entering the warehouse doors for the last time, JT picked up the kerosene cans and spread the fuel around the inside of the warehouse, including the pillow room. He moved back outside, dressed in the white pillowcases and blending in with the snow. He picked up his exceptional spear, lifted his head to the sky, and howled!

Duvall led his gang through the diminishing snow, cold and without hope. "Holy shit, look at that!" the outlaw riding next to him exclaimed. There was a huge plume of smoke off to his left.

"Come on," Duvall ordered. Ten minutes later, the gang approached the fire but backed off as their mounts shied away from the heat.

"Sir, maybe JT Thomas started this fire. I see some tracks leading into the woods, heading west," one of the men said.

Another outlaw volunteered, "I see tracks going east." Others rode up and reported tracks heading north and south. Duvall shook his head, thinking, *He knew exactly what he was doing. He's trying to divide us up, and it's going to work.*

"All right, let's split up in groups of two. If you find him, fire three shots and we will meet back here," Duvall ordered. The outlaws nodded grimly, and each pair took a trail.

≈ ≈ ≈ ≈ ≈

JT made his way down the tracks, picking up his supplies and securing one of the knives with a strip of pillowcase tied around his waist. He stopped just short of where his previous tracks ended, next to a huge fallen oak tree in a snow-covered clearing. He crossed over the log with the help of the spear, then replaced the snow that he knocked off the trunk and burrowed into the snow behind it.

JT waited patiently and was rewarded when he heard nearby voices. He peeked over the log and smiled, seeing two outlaws moving toward him. The first man had a Winchester in one hand and the reins in the other. He let him go by and, as the second rider rode near, he jumped up and pushed the man out of the saddle, making his horse bolt and his Winchester fly into the deep snow. JT threw his spear and smiled as he watched it pierce the first outlaw's back. His horse reared, throwing the man into the snow. JT jumped off the log just as the second outlaw was getting to his feet, struggling to remove his hammer strap. The man was having no luck since he was wearing thick winter gloves. JT landed on the man, drove him into the snow-covered ground, and held his blade to his throat.

"You make a noise and I will slit your damn throat. Do you understand?" he hissed.

The man nodded as JT took his gun and leveled it at him. JT chuckled, noting the man's build. "Well, I guess it's my lucky day! Tell you what—if you shuck off those clothes and do it fast, I may not skin you alive," he said, brandishing his knife. "Hand them over and be quick about it."

When the outlaw was completely naked, JT had him lie face down in the snow and knelt on the man's back. He tied his arms tightly behind him and loosely tied his ankles. Rolling him over, he gagged him and stood back. "Okay, get the hell out of here," JT exclaimed as he pointed down the trail. "And tell that no-good Duvall I'll be waiting for him up the mountain."

The man hurried down the snow-covered trail with a look of fear on his face. JT quickly put the man's warm clothes on, strapped on the gun and holster, and retrieved the Winchester from the snow. He headed toward the horse, grabbed the reins, and led him back to the log. He quickly stuffed the rest of the man's clothes and his supply pillowcases into the saddlebags, noting there was extra ammunition at the bottom. Mounting up, he replaced the rifle into its scabbard, pulled out his new Colt, and made his way to the first outlaw. Snow was beginning to cover him and the spear was still sticking out of his back.

JT dismounted, keeping the Colt trained on the man, then squatted down and rolled him over. The man was certainly dead, his glassy eyes staring at the winter sky. JT loosened the man's holster and took it, the pistol still strapped inside. Then after a bit of a chase through the deep snow, he caught the man's gelding. He stuffed the revolver into the saddlebags and tethered the horse to his new mount.

JT headed into the forest and back up the mountain toward his stash. Out of the corner of his eye he saw a red flash through the pine trees, and thought he heard the sound of sleigh bells.

Chapter Thirty

Will and Stiff headed for the Colorado town of Ashcroft and Cody Newton's cabin. They had decided they didn't want to deal with Snake Brill's mother any sooner than they had to. Besides, Ashcroft had a lawman and a hotel. They rode into town mid-afternoon, checked into the hotel, then went to the livery and arranged for their horses to be taken care of.

Directly across the street was the jail, and four doors down was the Red Door Saloon. "Well, what is your choice, Will? Jail or saloon?" Stiff asked.

Will nodded at the jail. "It's a bit early for a drink, so let's start with the sheriff."

The door to the jail was open and there was a napping deputy behind the desk. Stiff knocked loudly on the open door and the deputy bolted upright. "Whoa," he exclaimed. "Must have dozed off there for a moment. What can I do for you gents?"

"We are looking for the sheriff," Stiff said gruffly.

The deputy pointed across the street. "Oh, he's having a beer over at the saloon." He was fidgeting in his seat and red in the face.

Stiff headed over, but Will cocked his head and asked, "Something wrong, partner?"

"Oh, he doesn't like to see people sleeping on the job. He was in the Navy once and told me if you fell asleep on duty, they would flog you, or worse! But hell, I pulled the night shift last night and I ain't even being paid for today. I'm just filling in 'cause the other no-good deputy is sick with whiskey flu, if you know what I mean!"

Will held his hands out in a placating gesture. "Don't worry, the sheriff won't hear anything from us. If you're up and around later, come find us and I'll buy you a beer," he said, then turned and headed for the Red Door.

Will pushed through the saloon's bat wings, which were dark red as advertised. Stiff was standing next to the sheriff with a glass of beer in his hand. "I thought it was too early to drink!" Will said with a smirk.

Stiff pointed at the sheriff. "Well, the sheriff is buying us a round since I told him who we were looking for."

The sheriff held out his hand. "Sheriff Wyatt Earp," he said.

Will looked at Stiff as he shook the man's hand. "Really?"

The sheriff laughed. "Naw, I'm just pulling your leg. I'm Wyatt Tilly, and don't even comment on my last name. Sounds like an ugly whore, doesn't it?"

"Aw, that's not so bad. My partner's name is Stiff!" Will chuckled.

Tilly broke out into a roaring laugh and slapped his leg. "My God, that's hilarious! What, was your old man an undertaker?"

Will smiled and chuckled and Stiff didn't. "No," Stiff replied, "he was a sheriff in Wisconsin and he got killed by a bank robber."

Tilly stood up. "I'm sorry to hear that, and I meant no offense."

"None taken. Now how about I buy you a round, and you can tell us about Cody Newton and his brother."

"Oh yes, Turk and Cody. Hard to say which one's the bigger lowlife," Tilly said. "So, their cabin's about ten miles outside of town…"

≈ ≈ ≈ ≈ ≈

Will and Stiff headed toward the Newton cabin. Tilly had told them it was on a stream that was off the beaten path, next to a boulder the size of a small house. They dismounted at the beginning of a well-used trail and slowly made their way, Will carrying his Winchester and Stiff with his 50-caliber buffalo gun.

Seeing the cabin in the distance, they moved off the trail and into the woods. The place was well tended and looked solidly built. There was an outhouse near the creek and a small corral where four horses were eating hay in the snow. Smoke was coming out of the chimney.

Stiff whispered to Will, "I'll set up here. Why don't you make your way around the cabin and see if there is a back door?" Will nodded and disappeared into the trees.

Stiff propped his 50-caliber in a Y-shaped branch and focused on the front door. Meanwhile, the outhouse door opened and a man emerged, buckling his holster and tying a leather string to his right leg. Stiff smiled, noting that he must be an experienced gunfighter. Suddenly, the man stopped and looked toward the forest. He bolted for the door as Stiff's finger tightened on the buffalo gun's trigger. Stiff sighed and relaxed his finger. As of yet, he didn't know if this was Cody or Turk, and he wasn't going to shoot until he did.

Will scrambled up to him and dove to the ground just as a window shattered and a rifle shot echoed into the woods. Stiff knew he was fairly well hidden, but he grabbed his rifle anyway and dropped into the snow next to Will.

Stiff snorted. "Welcome back. What did you find back there?"

"Nothing. No back door and no windows," he said, as another shot hit a tree ten feet away from them.

Stiff nodded at a spot forty yards away. "Why don't you move over there? We can set up a crossfire."

As Will moved back into the forest and reappeared behind a snow-covered log, a voice came from the cabin. "Who the hell is out there?"

Will called out, "We are looking for Cody Newton!"

"He ain't here."

"Yeah, then why the hell are you shooting at us?"

There was a long pause. "I thought you was a deer."

"Yep, that's right, I'm a gol-darned deer. You killed me, so why don't you come out and gut me?"

Stiff laughed out loud. Two rifles opened fire at the log Will was hiding behind, peppering it and sending up plumes of snow. Stiff took aim at the rifle on the left and slowly squeezed the trigger. The 50-caliber spit out fire, smoke, and death, and he heard a scream from the cabin. "You killed Turk, you son of a bitch!"

Stiff had quickly moved ten yards to his left, burrowing into the snow. "Well, deer know how to shoot too!" Will said with a snort.

Cody screamed, "He was my only brother and he wasn't even wanted!"

"Deer me!" Will bellowed. Stiff frowned at him, and Will shrugged. "Bad joke?"

Stiff shouted out, "Cody Newton, we know you are in there and we are sorry about your brother, but you best come out with your hands on your head. Otherwise, we are gonna burn down the cabin around your ears."

"You wouldn't do that. This cabin was my brother's pride and joy!" Cody yelled.

"Well, he is surely dead, and if you were a good brother you would come out. Think about how he'd feel in heaven looking down and watching his nifty cabin burn to the ground."

A minute passed before the door opened and Cody walked out with his Winchester over his head. He threw it in the snow, then picked his Colt up by his finger and thumb and tossed it into the snow as well. Then he sat down on the snowy steps and wept.

Will and Stiff rode into Ashcroft and straight up to the sheriff's office. Cody had been silent on the ride in, clearly dejected and causing no trouble. The deputy stood up, looking a little alarmed. He called for the sheriff and Tilly emerged from the back. "So, you found him," he said. "Did his brother give you any trouble?"

Will deadpanned, "Naw, last time we saw him he was out huntin' deer." Stiff shook his head and Will laughed.

Chapter Thirty-One

The naked outlaw hobbled downhill to the smoldering warehouse fire and moved close, soaking in the warmth.

He was groaning to himself and cussing to beat the band. "Holy shit! Luke Biggins, what happened to you?" asked a voice from behind.

He looked over his shoulder, not wanting to turn around. "Well, I found that goddamned JT Thomas. He killed Sam and he took my goddamned clothes, and God damn it, I'm going to kill him. Twice!"

The outlaw dismounted, grabbed his blanket, and covered Luke. "I'm sorry to hear about Sam. He was a good shot," he said, firing off three shots to summon the rest of the gang.

≈≈≈≈≈

Duvall pulled up to the congregating outlaws, who had thrown tree branches on the dying warehouse fire to warm themselves. He was directed to Luke, who was sitting and shivering in a blanket. Duvall listened to his story and grimaced, seeing the discouraged look on the faces of his gang. He called three men over and said, "You stay with Luke and lend him some clothes and boots. I don't want him freezing to death. The rest of you, mount up. Thomas isn't getting away this time!"

He got on his horse and waved the men forward. Most followed him, but about half a dozen didn't.

Luke looked around at his cold and discouraged partners. He held his hands out to the fire. "I'm quittin'. This is bullshit, and I'm heading out! Anyone want to join me?" The outlaws nodded, one after another.

Chickens were striding around near the fire, and the outlaw who was still mounted smoothly shucked out his Colt and blew the head off of three of them. As the last one scurried away, the man shrugged. "Hell, that damn chicken looked sickly, so you should be thankin' me for that. Now, let's eat and get the hell out of here!"

$$\approx \approx \approx \approx \approx$$

JT moved through the forest and up the slope as quickly as possible. He stopped at a cave that was small and shallow, but it at least got him out of the snow. He left his new horses saddled, regretting that he had no food for them, and built a small fire. Sitting on a small boulder, he ate the cold chicken and boiled eggs he had brought along. He thought about making coffee, but decided he needed to put out the small fire before it attracted attention.

He made himself as comfortable as he could with the bedrolls and blankets, and spent a fitful night. At dawn, he continued up the mountain. He looked down the slope and was relieved to see that no one was following him. But his horses were struggling through the snow, so he finally dismounted and led them up the slope.

JT pushed on through the early afternoon until he recognized the spot where he had left his stash. JT smiled as he moved the saddlebags off the smaller horse and put them on the larger one. The animal was a sturdy gray quarter horse, nearly sixteen and a half hands tall and more sure-footed than his counterpart.

The snowfall stopped as he took out his knife and arduously dug a small pit in the ground. He periodically glanced down the slope, looking for his pursuers. It was hard work in the frozen ground, and he actually had to take off his winter coat to keep from sweating. Finally, the hole was deep enough, and he gingerly placed the rest of the dynamite in it. He then placed the coffee pot in the middle of the pit and chuckled to himself.

He mounted the large horse, leaving the smaller one tethered to a heavy rock. The sure-footed mount made his way slowly up the mountain, leaving tracks that a blind man could follow. JT reached down and patted its neck, gently kneeing him in the flank. "Okay boy, let's get the hell away from the dynamite," he said.

≈ ≈ ≈ ≈ ≈

Duvall and his cold, diminished gang made their way up the mountain, not even bothering to spread out. The fact that about a dozen men had apparently deserted them was not lost on the remaining outlaws. He was thinking about heading back down the mountain to regroup, or simply giving up the hunt, when he looked ahead and saw a horse standing about a hundred yards away. The gang pulled up around him. "Hey, that's Luke's Appaloosa!" one man exclaimed.

Duvall reached into his coat pocket, withdrew a stack of bills, and held it up over his head. "I'll pay two hundred dollars to the man brave enough to ride up there and check this out," he proclaimed.

The outlaws either looked away or hung their heads. "God damn it, I'll make it five hundred!" Duvall shouted.

The pockmarked, long-haired man who had been one of the last to join the gang raised his hand, saying, "I'll do it, but you all keep me covered."

Duvall nodded and handed the money to the man. The gang moved aside and each member raised a rifle as the outlaw rode slowly up the mountain. "What an idiot," a man near Duvall said with a snort.

The volunteer, Flynn Nacuna, held his Winchester at the ready as he climbed the mountainside. He was so skittish he took over fifteen minutes to get to the tethered horse.

Twenty yards from the site, he turned and yelled to the distant gang. "It's all clear! Come on up, and bring some dry branches for a fire. That goddamned Thomas left us some coffee!"

The gang rode up the steep slope. They worked in pairs, one man stopping occasionally to pick up a branch, while the man next to him shouldered his rifle and scanned the mountain. They gathered around Flynn, who was holding the wad of bills over his head. "Easiest money I ever made!" he grinned.

The gang dismounted as Flynn quickly crouched down and lit the fire. He grabbed his canteen and added water to the coffee pot, then put it close to the fire. As the men dug out their cups, Duvall backed away from the fire and motioned to Samson Nasle, one of Perez's right-hand men. As Nasle rode over, Duvall shook his head and whispered, "This doesn't smell right."

All hell broke loose as the fire pit exploded, sending outlaws and horses in bloody pieces. Dust and rock also exploded, creating a small avalanche. Nasle took the brunt of the explosion in the back and landed on Duvall, flattening him into the snow. Duvall couldn't hear his own screams as he pushed Nasle off.

He lay where he was for what seemed like an eternity with his eyes closed. Finally, he rolled over and looked at Nasle's dead body. His back was shredded, but what caught Duvall's attention was the fact that a baseball-sized rock was embedded in the back of his cranium. He bent over and vomited, then looked up in shock. The fire was gone; in its place was a large, smoking pit and a scene of total devastation. His gang and all the horses were blown to smithereens, along with his stash of Marcus Payne's money.

Duvall stood on the mountain slope, tilted his head back, and screamed. "God damn you, JT Thomas! GOD DAMN YOU!"

JT heard the explosion and smiled. He turned his horse down the slope and headed for Point Stevens Pass. By dusk, he had reached the forest and made camp there for the night, heating up the rest of the chicken and opening a can of peaches. After the meager meal, he wrapped himself in the bedrolls and blankets. As he drifted off to sleep, he heard a loud purring and smiled. *Hello there, Red.*

At dawn, JT made a light breakfast and packed up. He looked into the woods for a red flash, but it did not come.

Chapter Thirty-Two

JT rode into Point Stevens Pass and headed to the livery. Buck greeted him with his booming voice. "My friend JT, it is SO good to see you!"

JT dismounted and shook Buck's hand. "Good to see you as well, Buck. How are things here?" he inquired.

"Things are okay. None of the outlaws came back, so I'm guessing you took care of them."

JT nodded. "Yeah, most of them, anyway."

Buck grinned widely as he took JT's new horse. "So, another new horse. Do you just pluck them off trees?" he asked, laughing.

"No, I actually earned this one, and I'm thinking I'll keep him. He is as sure-footed as I've ever seen."

Bucked nodded. "Well, I'll take good care of him."

As JT headed toward the hotel, Buck called after him. "Say, you may want to touch base with Gregor Nelson. It seems you got richer while you were being hunted by those darn outlaws!"

JT waved over his shoulder without turning around. *Richer?*

He walked into the hotel after greeting the town's protectors, now employees of his new agency. The desk clerk greeted him and handed him a key to his suite. "Welcome back, Mr. Thomas," the man said, smiling.

JT nodded and started up the stairs, but turned back. "Could you get someone to go get the bank manager and have him come to my room?" he asked politely.

The man saluted. "I will do it myself, Mr. Thomas."

JT entered the suite. He smiled at the sight of the large bathtub in the corner, sat down, and started to undress. He was down to his pants and long johns when he heard a knock on the door. "Come on in, it's not locked," he said, grabbing the outlaw's Colt and placing it on his lap.

The door opened and the bank manager stuck his head in. "Hello, Mr. Thomas. I'm so glad you are back safe and sound. All of us were worried about you!" he stated, not seeming to notice JT's state of partial dress.

JT put the gun away and motioned for him to sit. "I'm going to need about a hundred dollars since I lost what I took with me," he said. The banker nodded as if this was not unusual. "Also, I'm going to need the manager of the mercantile shop to pick out a couple of new sets of clothes and a winter coat, hat, and gloves. Also a new Stetson; he will know which one I'm talking about. He knows my sizes."

The banker nodded. "I will bring the clothes over myself and the money as well, Mr. Thomas. You are our number one client by far, and we would be delighted to serve you in any way."

JT got up from the comfortable chair he had plopped down on and shook the man's hand. "Thank you very much, I surely appreciate that. Would you also ask the desk clerk to bring me hot water, soap, and towels for a bath?"

The banker nodded and opened the door. "I'll tell him. Oh, and would you like a bottle of Scotch?"

JT grinned. "That would be wonderful!" he exclaimed.

The banker paused at the door. "By the way, I have sent your 'reward canceled' poster to every bank in Colorado with a notice that they need to put it up in their lobby. And believe me, they will do it. Your newfound wealth is making the other bankers drool with envy! In addition to that, I am holding the map and other assets Mr. Nelson retrieved from your cave in my safe. They are accessible to you any time you would like to view them." And then he left with a broad smile on his face.

The bath provisions were delivered within minutes, along with JT's favorite whiskey. He locked the door, poured himself a drink, and crawled into the hot bath with a sigh. As he sipped his Scotch, he thought, *My God, it is truly nice to be rich. And I had forgotten all about the treasure map!*

Chapter Thirty-Three

Duvall limped, tired and nearly frozen, into St. Elmo. He climbed the stairs of a small boarding house and rang the bell. A white-haired woman stepped through the back door and behind the reception desk. Her smile quickly faded. "Oh my, sir, you are hurt!" she exclaimed.

Duvall leaned heavily on the desk, pulled the only remaining money from his winter coat, and put it on the desk. "I'd like a room …" he started, then collapsed in a heap on the floor.

He woke up in bed with the concerned woman sitting in a chair across the room and a man with a stethoscope standing over him. The woman stood up, came over to the bed, and gripped the doctor's elbow. "Is he going to be all right?" she asked.

The doctor nodded. "He is going to be fine; nothing your soup and a warm room won't cure." He nodded at Duvall. "You were lucky you didn't freeze out there."

Duvall sat up and nodded. "Where am I?" he inquired.

"Well, you're in St. Elmo, and you are lucky to be alive."

Duvall lay back in the comfortable bed. *Lucky? That's a bad joke.*

≈≈≈≈≈

JT's new clothes were a little loose fitting after his mountain-climbing excursion. He slowly climbed down the stairs and beckoned to the clerk. "Any idea where I could find Gregor Nelson?"

The man nodded. "Yes, he checked out yesterday and is staying at Emma's boarding house."

JT tipped his new Stetson and made his way to Emma's. As he approached, he stopped and admired the new structure. It was painted yellow with white trim. Out front was a white picket fence and a portico leading to the front door. JT climbed the porch stairs and opened the windowed double doors, triggering a small bell. Inside the entrance was a high ceiling and a small reception desk. There also was a leather couch and two matching chairs that looked awfully comfortable, tired as he was.

As he stepped up to the reception desk, a door opened and Emma stepped out, followed by Gregor Nelson. Emma hurried around the reception desk and enveloped JT in a massive hug. "Oh my God, JT, it is so good to see you!" she said as she stepped back.

Gregor smiled broadly and shook JT's hand. "Good to see you, boss!" he exclaimed.

JT smiled and pointed at a chair. "Mind if I sit down? It's been a long day."

Emma quickly grabbed JT's elbow and guided him to the chair. "Can I get you some water or some coffee? Or something stronger?" she inquired.

JT shook his head. "I'm fine, just tired and hungry."

"Well then, let's feed you! The café isn't open but I have steaks, potatoes, and carrots. If you like I can whip up some sweet rolls too. You and Gregor catch up and I'll get busy in the kitchen," she said, as she locked the front door and put up a closed sign.

An hour later, they finished the hearty meal. "Emma, that was the best meal I have ever had. Thank you!" JT said quietly.

Emma beamed and refilled his coffee cup. "Thank you so much, JT. I've never seen you eat so much before."

"Well, I didn't get a lot to eat out there, except some fresh chicken and eggs," he said with a smile.

Gregor spoke up. "Tell us all about it."

"Well, it was an interesting adventure, but I'm not sure even Annabelle would have enjoyed it." JT began the long story, leaving out the parts with the cougar. Gregor and Emma sat rapt in their chairs as JT described the harrowing events. "And that is a summary of the last week or so," he said with a tired chuckle.

Emma responded, "My God, JT, that's the most incredible story I've ever heard. Naked and pillows and dynamite! Incredible. I'm just so glad you are okay!"

Gregor smiled. "That is quite a story, and I'm thinking Annabelle actually might have enjoyed it. I've got a bit of a story to tell too, but I think you might need a long winter's nap first."

Emma chimed in, "Oh yes, your room is all ready. Let me scoot up and put sheets on the bed. I think you are going to love the room."

"Boss, let's have dinner at the hotel café this evening and I'll fill you in. Emma has been working her fingers to the bone and she deserves a night out," Gregor said.

JT nodded. "How about if we invite the Doc, Dawn, and Buck from the livery?"

Gregory nodded. Soon, Emma returned and led a sleepy JT up to his new suite. "This is wonderful, Emma. It's just perfect," JT mumbled as he collapsed on the bed.

As Emma covered him with a quilt and quietly left, JT briefly opened his eyes and looked around the beautiful room. "If only Annabelle were here," he whispered with a sigh, then promptly fell asleep.

≈ ≈ ≈ ≈ ≈

Will and Stiff rode into St. Elmo, Colorado in search of Snake Brill, hoping to avoid his mother if they could. They were tired, thirsty, and hungry and headed straight to the saloon.

The place was nearly empty so they took a table with a view of the door. Stiff pointed at the beer spigot, holding up two fingers. The bartender smiled, drew two glasses, and set them on the table.

Will proceeded to drain his glass as Stiff took a deep gulp, then pointed at his glass and held two fingers in the air. The barkeep set another round in front of the dusty riders. Stiff looked at Will. "I didn't need another one," he said flatly.

Will downed his second glass as quickly as the first, then pulled Stiff's beer toward him. "Who the hell said it's for you?" he asked, with a twinkle in his eye. "Hey barkeep, have any food back there? We're mighty hungry," he said, and let out a burp. "Excuse me," he said to no one in particular.

"Supper ain't until 4:30, but I've got ham, cheddar cheese, and some sweet onion back there. I can make you a sandwich if you like," the man replied.

"That sounds mighty good. I'll take two of them and another beer."

Stiff nodded at the barkeep. "I'll take just one, with extra onions. Also, two fingers of good rum if you have it, and another beer before my partner drinks it all," he said, shaking his head at Will, who sat with a loopy grin.

After wolfing the sandwiches down, they motioned the bartender back over. "How was the sandwich, gents?" he asked.

"Good," Stiff replied. "Not enough onion, but good. Say, we are looking for Snake Brill. Do you know where we might find him?"

The bartender frowned. "Yeah, he lives a couple of streets over with that damn feisty mother of his. But I wouldn't go over there—that woman is as mean as a starving rattler. I'd just wait here since he usually comes in for supper and a drink or two. His momma can't cook for a damn so he usually dines here."

Stiff looked at Will, who nodded affirmatively. The bartender glanced at the empty glasses. "You want another round?" he inquired.

The partners shook their heads. "Naw, but make us a pot of coffee," Stiff said.

By the time the coffee arrived, the saloon was filling up. Snake Brill pushed his way through the doors and made his way to the bar. The bartender put a glass of beer and a shot of rye in front of him, nodding to Will and Stiff. "How's it going, Snake?" he asked, as Snake threw back the rye.

"Not so well. My damn mother is driving me crazy. She has a honey-do list longer than my arm and she is the biggest nag I've ever known. No wonder my old man blew his brains out! Hell, I'm thinking of doing the same thing," he said, and took a deep pull on his beer. "Or either kill her, but I think she is too damn mean to die," he said with a half laugh.

Stiff stood up, removing the hammer strap from his Smith & Wesson Model 3. "Hey bartender, buy Snake another round on us," he said.

Snake turned to face him with a frown on his face. "I can buy my own drinks, stranger, and only my friends call me Snake."

"Ok, so what would you prefer to be called?"

"Prefer? Prefer? I'll tell you what. You can call me Sir," he growled, as his hand moved to his revolver.

"Hey, how did you get the name Snake anyway?" Will asked.

"Who the hell are you?"

Will chuckled. "Well, my name is Will, but sometimes I go by Deer."

"Deer? What kind of name is that?"

"Hey, my partner is called Stiff. What do you think about that?"

Snake looked at both of them and shook his head. "Well, I think I'm gonna kill both of you. And my friends call me Snake 'cause I can snake this Colt out faster than anybody!" he said, as he went for his pistol. He got it out of the holster and had the hammer halfway down when he felt a thump in his chest. Surprised, he looked down to see his crimson blood quickly staining his shirt. "Son of a bitch," he said, as his gun dropped to the floor. Snake quickly followed, bouncing the back of his head off the bar and landing on his gun. He lay convulsing for a minute before he gave off his death rattle.

Will looked at Stiff. "Are you slowing down?"

Stiff holstered his six-shooter. "Yeah, not enough practice."

The bartender reached over and picked up Snake's beer glass, drained it, and wiped his hand across his mouth. "Hey, waste not, want not," he said. "That son of a bitch never left a tip in his life!"

Since there was no sheriff in town, Snake's body had been taken to the livery for Will and Stiff to pick up in the morning. They had a good breakfast in the saloon, scrambled eggs with ham bits and fried potatoes, then said goodbye to the bartender and strode to the livery. The owner was waiting for them with Snake's dead body tied over his horse. His helper had their own mounts saddled and ready. Stiff nodded to him and climbed into the saddle. Will pitched the livery owner a five-dollar gold piece and peeked into Snake's saddlebags. He closed them quickly with a smile on his face.

The livery owner came over and grabbed Snake's horse, holding on to the reins. "Not enough," said the man. "I need fifty dollars."

Will sat there with his mouth open, not saying a word. Stiff was almost out the door, but turned around and rode back into the barn. "What did you say?" he asked, scowling.

"I said I need fifty dollars. That is Snake's horse, and I figure you're a stealing him. And horse stealing is a hanging offense around here!" he exclaimed.

Stiff looked over at Will, who was shaking his head. "How the hell do you figure we are stealing the horse? You can plainly see Snake is riding him, so we ain't stealing him," Stiff responded.

The livery owner shook his head. "Nope, he is dead and has no say in the manner, so you're stealing the man's horse, plain and simple."

"Well, why don't we go settle this with the sheriff?"

"We ain't got a sheriff and you know it. You are hauling Snake away to collect the reward, which I happen to know is five hundred dollars. So I want fifty bucks."

Will began to laugh, as did the livery helper and then the owner, but not Stiff. "What's so darn funny?" Stiff said to Will.

"Oh, pay him, the man has a point," Will grinned.

"I certainly will not!" Stiff exclaimed.

Will reached into his shirt pocket and took out a small wad of bills. He peeled off five ten-dollar bills and handed them to the owner, accepting Snake's reins in return. The liveryman tipped his cap to Will. "Nice doing business with you," he said, scowling at Stiff.

As the two partners rode slowly out of the livery, they heard the loud boom of a shotgun. The livery owner stuck his head out of the door and cried out, "That's Snake's mother, and she is hell on wheels with that Greener. I'd get the hell out of here if I were you!" They kicked their horses in the flanks and took off as if they had been shot out of a cannon, with Snake and his high-priced horse right behind. They heard another boom and ducked, coaxing their horses into a full gallop.

"You killers!" they heard Snake's mother scream. "Who's going to help me with my to-do list?" Peering over their shoulders, they were glad to see she didn't have a horse.

When they were safely a mile out of town, Stiff confronted his partner. "What the hell was that all about with the fifty dollars? That was just blackmail!" he said angrily.

Will laughed. "Well, buddy, if you'd bothered to look in Snake's saddlebags, you'd have seen his share of the bank money. And I figure we can get thirty bucks at least for that fine horse and another fifteen for his fancy Mexican saddle. Not to mention ten bucks for his Winchester. So, I'm guessing we come out five dollars ahead!" he said with a grin.

And Stiff nearly smiled.

Chapter Thirty-Four

Duvall sat up in his boarding house bed and finished his chicken soup. He tilted the bowl to get the last drop, then handed the spoon and bowl to Mary Ann, the elderly proprietor. "Well, how was it?" she inquired anxiously.

Duvall smiled. "Mary Ann, that was wonderful! That was the best chicken soup I have ever tasted. I'm not kidding you; it was superb!"

Mary Ann beamed. "Would you like more?"

Duvall laughed. "No, three bowls is my limit."

"Well, there is more on the stove and the doctor says you can have solid food next. But I must tell you I don't have much in stock. Since the new hotel went up with their fancy café, my business has fallen off a cliff," she said, frowning.

"Well, you take twenty dollars and go get some groceries," Duvall said, pointing at the stack of bills on the dresser.

Mary Ann stood up with the bowl and spoon in hand. "Thank you so much, that's mighty nice of you. What would you like for your first meal?"

"How about a thick steak and taters for both of us, and whatever's fresh in the way of vegetables?"

"Fine! Why don't you take a nap? I'll clean up the kitchen and head over to the mercantile shop."

As she turned to leave, Xavier lay back down and put his head on the pillow. "Ah, Mary Ann, I don't like carrots."

"Then we won't have carrots," she said with a giggle.

Duvall looked up at the ceiling, thinking about his mother. His mother Sissy was no cook; she couldn't even boil an egg. She was a prostitute in New York City, so his father could have been anyone. But they were never poor and she took good care of him, at least as well as she could being out all night earning a living. Xavier smiled at the memory, then turned on his side and fell asleep.

≈≈≈≈≈

JT walked down the steps of the brand-new boarding house, noting the detail and obvious effort that went into the design. He rang the small bell on the reception counter and smiled when Emma and Gregor came through the door. "Did you have a good nap?" Emma asked.

"Absolutely. I must tell you; this place is extraordinary. You should be congratulated on your attention to detail," JT said.

Emma blushed and took Gregor's arm. "Well, I wanted to get it right. Thanks to your generosity and Gregor's skill, I think it turned out ok. And we'll have the grand opening real soon now!"

"Good! Now let's go eat. I could eat a horse, uncooked!" he exclaimed, as he opened the boarding house door for Emma.

They made their way to the hotel café. Dawn and Doctor DeWitt were there waiting, along with Buck. And, lo and behold, he had a coat and tie on! Dawn gave JT a long hug. The doctor shook his hand and patted him on the back, while Buck simply stood there, embarrassed. As the group sat down, JT looked at Buck. "Thanks for joining us, Buck. It's nice to see you out of the livery," he said.

Buck looked around the table sheepishly. "Well, ah, thanks for inviting me. I normally take my meals over at the saloon, but this is mighty nice," he said, looking at the white table cloth and the fine table setting. "Mighty nice."

JT smiled. "And boy, you clean up pretty well for an old guy!" he said with a chuckle.

Dawn leaned over to Buck. "Don't mind him. I think you're a fine figure of a man," she said. And Buck smiled.

The waiter arrived and explained the specials, which were baked chicken with garlic and sherry or center cut pork chops and white rice, cooked in beef broth. As he took the drink orders and departed, Dawn turned to JT. "I'm so glad you are back. We were on pins and needles while you were gone."

JT smiled and replied, "I'm mighty glad to be back, and thanks for your concern. It's good to have friends like you."

DeWitt spoke up. "Hear, hear. So, tell us all about it!"

JT chuckled and started the story again. When it was through, everyone sat silently.

It was Buck who spoke up first, raising his glass. "That is an incredible story. And all I can say is good for you Mr. Thomas, they all got what they deserved!"

"That they did!" DeWitt proclaimed, as the party clinked glasses and smiled at JT.

The meal was pronounced delicious by all. As they finished, DeWitt asked the waiter if the bar had that new French liquor called Grand Marnier. "Yes sir!" the man replied. "Glasses for all?" DeWitt smiled and nodded.

The waiter returned with the drinks and DeWitt said, "I think you will like this. It is really orange cognac and is very tasty. If you don't care for it, let me know and I'd be happy to drink it for you!" Everyone laughed and took sips, nodding appreciatively.

Gregor cleared his throat and addressed JT. "Well, I have some good news for you. While you were out having your pillow adventure, I stopped at the cave and ran into your old nemesis, Jean Cantrell. It was a coincidence, but let me tell you what happened…"

The table listened quietly to Gregor's remarkable story. "…and I picked up a few nice pieces from the gold seam and went out the back of the cave," he said. He reached into his pocket, produced a small piece of rock with a streak of gold that sparkled under the light, and passed it over to JT, "So, boss, it seems like you keep getting richer and richer," he said with a chuckle.

JT sat stunned, looking at the gleaming stone. After a minute, he simply nodded and passed it around the table.

"As soon as I got back, I sent a wire to our mining engineer in Golden. I told him to set up whatever and whoever he needs to run a gold mine and to survey the rest of the mountain. We will lay claim to as much as the government will allow. It will cost a bit, but I promise it will be well worth it," Gregor concluded.

JT called the waiter over and got another round served. He stood up and toasted his friends. "Thanks to all of you, and especially to my friend and partner Mr. Gregor Nelson. Gregor, I truly appreciate that you put yourself in harm's way for me. I would like you to share equally with me whatever comes out of the mountain."

Emma grabbed Gregor's elbow and nearly cried as Gregor beamed at JT. "Thank you very much, boss. As usual, your generosity astounds me."

DeWitt stood up and raised his glass. "I was planning on paying for this Grand Mariner, but now I think I'll let my rich friend Gregor pay!"

"Hear, hear!" everyone agreed, laughing.

Drew Morrow set the letter from his friend Morton Bernstein on his desk and smiled as he read.

Dear Drew,

I hope this correspondence finds you well.

Thank you for all of your assistance with the Barnabas Poe situation. I have received wires and a letter from my former employee Gregor Nelson, who speaks highly of you and your outstanding job of shutting down Barnabas Poe.

I am writing to you with good news regarding Mr. Marcus Payne. My dear friend Superior Court Judge Peter Collins has reviewed the conspiracy between Payne, Duvall, and Poe regarding the wanted poster that you included in your last communication. I am delighted to report that control of Mr. Payne's assets has been transferred to his daughter Madeline, who may use them as she sees fit.

Finally, please thank the governor for his invaluable assistance.

I hope to see you on your next trip to New York.

Sincerely,

Morton Bernstein, Esq.

P.S. I am sending a copy of this letter to Gregor Nelson, who has decided to stay in Colorado and is now employed by Mr. JT Thomas. I understand he is smitten with a fine woman named Emma and is thinking of marriage.

Drew stood up from his desk and stretched, looking out his office window. Poe was not only disgraced but also disbarred for life. His assistant had left him and come forward with some sordid details about the former attorney's activities. Numerous criminals had been placed under arrest and Poe was in the city jail on a suicide watch.

Drew looked at the letter and laughed. *God must hate slippery attorneys!*

Chapter Thirty-Five

Duvall woke up from his nap and got dressed, pocketing his money and buckling on his gun belt. He wandered into the kitchen where the elderly Mary Ann was busy with the meal. She looked over her shoulder and smiled. "Well, you certainly look better."

Duvall nodded. "It was the chicken soup," he said with a grin. "Well, that and a good night's sleep for the first time in a long while."

"Supper will be ready in twenty minutes. Would you like a cup of coffee or something stronger?"

"Something stronger would be dandy. What do you have?"

Mary Ann knelt down and pulled a nearly-full bottle of bourbon out of a low cupboard and passed it to him. "This was my late husband's. He liked a shot or two before supper."

"Well, he certainly had excellent taste!" Duvall exclaimed, as he glanced at the label.

Mary Ann handed him a small glass. "This was Mason's glass. Please help yourself."

Duvall poured himself two fingers. "Are you going to join me?"

"Oh my, no. The hard stuff just doesn't appeal to me. But I will join you with a glass of port after the meal is done!" she exclaimed.

Duvall nodded and sipped his bourbon. As he watched her prepare the meal, his stomach growled.

"That was simply wonderful," he stated, after the meal was over. He patted his full stomach.

Mary Ann looked up and smiled. "I'm glad you liked it." She cleaned up the kitchen as she sipped on her port. She looked over at the content man in her kitchen. "I couldn't help noticing a badge in your shirt pocket. Are you a sheriff?"

Xavier smiled. "Yes, I was for a long time, in New York City."

"Well, Colorado must be completely different than New York!"

"Oh, as different as night and day. But I'll tell you what, I really like it here. Folks are friendly and relaxed, not up in your face like in New York."

"Hmm, I never thought about that. I was born and raised here and never saw a reason to go anywhere else. Of course, we really didn't have money to travel."

Mary Ann finished cleaning up, freshened up her port, and sat across from Duvall. "You know, we have an opening for a sheriff here. The last one just disappeared. He went out at night looking for some rustlers and never came back."

Duvall frowned. "I'm sorry to hear that."

"Well, the job's been open for quite some time and I know Mayor Erv is anxious to fill the position. Once folks know a town doesn't have a lawman, unsavory characters drift right in and raise holy hell—pardon my French!"

Duvall laughed out loud. "Well, I might be interested. Where can I find this Mayor Erv?"

"Oh, he is bound to be over at Timbuck's Saloon, drinking and playing poker."

Xavier finished his drink and pinned his badge to his shirt pocket. "Okay, I think I'll go see the man and see what he's got to offer."

≈ ≈ ≈ ≈ ≈

Gregor Nelson sat in the lobby of Emma's boarding house reading aloud his copy of Bernstein's letter to Drew Morrow, but leaving out the part about marriage.

"Why, that is the best news I've had in a while!" JT exclaimed.

Emma looked up from her paperwork. "It surely is, Gregor, and I'm proud of the way you handled that."

Gregor nodded. "All's well that ends well! And with Payne cut off from his money he certainly can't continue the hunt for you, JT."

"I guess not, but I'm betting there are still some posters up," JT replied.

"Yes, but probably not as many as you think. I sent the new posters to darn near every town in Colorado. Will Benjamin and Stiff Digs are still out there distributing the replacements."

JT got up and refilled his coffee cup from the pot on the reception counter. "Yeah, I guess you are right. So, when do you think they are coming back? I'd like to include them in the meeting about starting our own detective agency."

Emma looked up. "What a wonderful idea! Those Pinkertons are now cozied up to the darn robber barons. I hear they're beating up and killing union members."

Gregor nodded. "That's true. It's one of the reasons I left, and a lot of the men we recruited did as well. Lots of Pinkerton agents' fathers are in unions!"

JT frowned. "That's not good. Besides, Pinkerton needs a little competition, especially in New Mexico and along the Arizona border. That is lawless territory and something needs to be done about it. I'd like to spend some of my newfound wealth and ramp it up quickly. Gregor, I'd like you to be in charge. I was impressed with Will and Stiff, and I think they'd make good right-hand men, but that decision will be up to you. We can talk salary later, but I think you will like the figure I have in mind. So, what do you say?"

"I say that is the best offer I've ever. I have one caveat, though. I'll need to stay here in Point Stevens Pass to be near Emma."

Emma blushed and nodded her head vigorously.

"That won't be a problem," JT replied. "In fact, I'd like you to ride herd on the new gold mine as well. You'll be mighty busy, but you'll also have free rein."

Gregor stood up and leaned forward to shake JT's hand. "Well then, you have got a deal."

JT grinned. "That's wonderful, but before you accept, I need to tell you that I'm headed to Arizona to start a ranch near my sister and her husband's place. My mother is out there with them, and I'd like to spend some time with her before she passes."

"Good for you!" Emma exclaimed. "Maybe we will come to visit once you're set up. It gets cold here in the winter!"

Gregor laughed. "That it does. Perhaps you could open another office of our agency since you are going to be close to New Mexico."

JT clapped him on the back. "Ah, great minds think alike. I was thinking that very thing."

Chapter Thirty-Six

Jean Cantrell rode into Bisby, a fairly large town with four saloons. Two of them offered womanly services to horny cowboys with money to spend. She rode up to the biggest, a place called The Lone Star, and dismounted. Her tired horse drank from the trough out front as she stepped through the doors. The place was nearly empty since it was mid-morning and they apparently did not serve breakfast. The bartender looked up as she entered. "Hey, no women in here, pretty lady!" he exclaimed.

Jean gave him her best smile. "Well, I'm here to apply for a job."

The man stopped putting the glasses away. "Really? You don't look like a whore."

Jean stopped in front of him. "Oh, but I am, and I can run a faro game with the best of them, too!"

The man chuckled. "I guess I don't doubt it. Let me take you to the manager."

Jean curtsied, even though she was wearing jeans. "I would appreciate it, kind sir."

The bartender knocked on the office door and a gruff voice called out, "Who is it?"

"It's Phil," the bartender responded. "I've got a pretty woman here who says she is an experienced soiled dove and knows how to hold down a faro table."

The door was unlocked and Jean looked at the shortest man she had ever seen. He was no taller than four feet and had the head of a grown man. He waved Jean in, pointing to a chair in front of his desk. "Thanks Phil, I'll take it from here," he said.

Jean sat down on the proffered chair as the small man made his way behind his desk. "So, little lady, is what Phil says true?" he asked.

Jean stood up, seductively removed all her clothes, and moved behind the desk. She knelt down next to the dwarf, rubbed his crotch, and unbuttoned his pants. "My, my," she said, looking down. "What a big boy you are!"

She proceeded to make the small man very happy. When she was done, she returned to the chair, still totally naked. "So, am I hired?"

The man simply nodded.

Duvall stood at Timbuck's bar, sipping a whiskey and chatting with the owner. "Your name is Tim, so why name your saloon Timbuck's?"

Tim stroked his bushy beard. "Simple. When I opened this place, I was hoping to make big bucks."

Duvall chuckled. "How's that working out for you?"

"Well, if more folks ordered the good stuff it would help. But I'm doing okay with all these new drifters coming in here since the sheriff got his neck stretched."

"I heard was he was out hunting rustlers and just didn't come back, That right?"

Tim chuckled quietly. "Oh, he didn't come back, but he surely got his neck stretched. See those two men in the corner drinking rotgut?"

"Yeah. What about them?"

"They are two of the rustlers he was after. And I got my information right from the horse's mouth, so to speak."

Duvall smiled. "Hey, hand me another glass." He took it and picked up his bottle, making his way over to the mayor, who was playing poker with some locals. He took a chair, filled the extra glass, and handed it to Erv. The mayor turned to Duvall and pitched his losing hand onto the table.

"Well thank you kindly, sir," he said, as he picked up the whiskey and threw it down his throat all at once. "Aw, that is might tasty liquor. I haven't been able to afford that in quite a while." He looked down at Duvall's shirt, noticing the sheriff's badge. Duvall refilled his glass, but this time the mayor sipped it. He stood up and said, "Deal me out," then picked up his drink and headed to an empty corner table.

The two men sat down. "Name's Erv, and I'm the mayor here. He nodded at the badge. "I haven't seen you around these parts, so where are you a sheriff?"

Duvall sipped his whiskey. "Used to be in New York, but business brought me west and I'm now looking for a job. Mary Ann over at the boarding house says you may have an opening."

Erv nodded, threw back his drink, and poured himself another. "Well, she is right. It pays fifty dollars a month, three squares a day, and you can live in the jailhouse."

Duvall cocked his head. "The money's okay, but I'm gonna need a paid room over at Mary Ann's boarding house. And I get ninety percent of any bounty money I collect."

Erv stood up. "I'll be right back." He went back to the card table, bent over, and had a discussion with the three other players. As Duvall watched, all of the players nodded and Erv made his way back to the table.

"That's the town council over there. We say yes, but we get thirty percent of the take on wanted men," he said.

Duvall filled up both of their glasses and held one out. "Make it twenty percent and you have a deal," he said with a smirk.

The mayor laughed and slapped his knee, then threw back his whiskey. "All right, you have a deal," he said. They shook hands. "You are now on the payroll." He looked over at the two rustlers in the corner. "Now, first order of business…"

Duvall smiled and tossed back his drink. "Yep, I know them. Tim pointed them out to me. Do you care whether I take them in dead or alive?"

"Don't make no difference to me. Wanted poster says dead or alive, $500 each."

Duvall slipped off his hammer strap, pulled out his Colt, and filled the cylinder. He poured himself a drink but let it sit. "Save that for me; I'll be back in a flash," he said, with a half laugh.

He strode quickly over to the rustlers, who were so inebriated they didn't even notice him standing at their table. "Hello gents," Duvall said as they looked up, spotting the badge. "No need to get up!" he said, as he drew his Colt and fired a shot into each man's chest and another into their faces. Their heads hit the table, which soon became covered with blood.

Duvall reloaded his gun, leaving one chamber empty. He spun around and returned to his table, picked up the glass and threw the tasty liquor down his throat.

"I guess both of us made some money already!" he said to the grinning mayor, then turned and headed for the door. "Tim, I'll go fetch the undertaker and somebody to clean this mess up." Tim nodded, open-mouthed and wide-eyed.

He walked down the saloon steps. *I think I'm gonna like it here!*

Chapter Thirty-Seven

The saloon was jumping as Jean stood at the faro table in a private room where only high rollers were allowed. She was in her element, having enlisted Taylor, the bar owner, as her accomplice in a crooked scheme involving a device called a sandbox and a specially prepared deck. Some cards had been "sanded" or roughened on one or both sides while others, which are intended to "tell," were left smooth. The rough cards would cling together, and any card that sat atop the smooth face of the "tell card" would slip easily and alert Jean, who would smile and declare herself the winner. It was a cheat that had served her well in the past.

Her current pigeon, Ceros T. McGriff, was a portly, nearly bald man with a squeaky voice. He was also no less than the local bank president. He was drinking so heavily and was so smitten with Jean that he cared little about his losses, though she figured he would feel different in the morning when he woke up with an empty wallet and a whopping hangover.

McGriff turned out his pockets. "Well Jean, looks like you cleaned me out again. How about you and I go upstairs and play jig jig again?" he said, with a drunken leer on his red face.

Jean displayed her most charming smile. "Ceros, you just plumb wore me out the last time. It's past your bedtime too, and I bet your wife is waiting for you to get home."

The banker sighed. "You're right, my little honey bunch. I guess I'll see you next week."

Jean led him weaving to the door and passed him to a very large bouncer named Lester, who by now knew the drill. "Walk him home and don't leave until he is in the house," she told him.

Lester nodded and took the banker's elbow. "Come right this way, Mr. McGriff. We will get you home." He winked at Jean and went through the saloon door.

Jean turned and saw Taylor pointing to her room at the top of the stairs, with a bottle of his private reserve Scotch in hand. She smiled weakly and made her way up the stairs. She had been on her feet, or her back, since a late breakfast at the café and was not looking forward to spending more time with Taylor. It had been over a month since she stepped into the Lone Star, and the whoring was wearing her down. Jean opened the door to her tiny room and sighed. *Honey bunch?*

But she had a plan to get back to what she really loved. She was going to use Mr. Ceros T. McGriff to help her rob his own bank. She knew his wife was going to visit her son in St. Louis for the holidays, and Mr. Banker would be all hers for a week. Soon she would be free of all this!

JT entered the hotel café and greeted Gregor, Stiff, Will, and seven other former Pinkertons agents. He had reserved the place for the first employee meeting of his new investigative agency, and this was the first time they had been in the same room together. Gregor stood up and clanked on his empty coffee mug with his spoon. "Good afternoon, men. I'd say good afternoon gentlemen, but I know you too well," he said with a grin. The room exploded in laughter.

"I take it you are all happy with the terms of employment?" The men nodded and smiled at JT. "Good. I have hand-picked you to start this fledgling company for numerous reasons. I have seen that you are tough but fair. You can be compassionate, but also mean and nasty when needed." He looked across the table at a trim man in his forties with a heavy afternoon shadow. "Especially B.J.," he said.

The men laughed. "Got that right!" one man exclaimed, as B.J. smiled and nodded. Gregor held his hand up in the air and the room quieted immediately.

"You are the core group and will be relied upon to set an example for the numerous men and women we will be adding to your ranks." Gregor continued. "All of you have different talents that we will utilize to the utmost, but you also have one trait in common, and it is why you are here and not still working for the Pinks." He looked each man in the eye. "Every one of you has good values and a code you live by. I've seen it in every one of you. You got into this line of work because you believe in justice, and because you want to protect people who need it. Well, that's why JT started this agency and why I picked you to be in it."

He moved in closer. "Some of you left good friends at the Pinkertons, and I know you wondered why they weren't given a chance to join us. I know because some of you have talked to me about it. But those men, talented as they are, don't have the core values to be a representative of our new agency. But you men have what it takes and will make good, solid decisions. You will be paired up and given assignments in Nevada, Arizona, and New Mexico. Especially New Mexico," he said, as heads nodded knowingly.

"Our first targets will be wanted men who are the worst of the worst. Rapists, murderers, and bank robbers head the list. We won't waste our time on the small fry, though if you find one in your daily excursions you can give them a piece of your mind and maybe a good thrashing." The men chuckled appreciatively.

"But for the most part, we pursue men wanted dead or alive. And let me make this clear: we don't do alive. I reiterate, these men are the worst of the worst and I don't want you to be molly-coddling evil outlaws. Shoot 'em where they stand and end their despicable disgusting lives. You will thank me for that order -- and it is an order. You don't have to feed a dead man or untie him so he can do his business if he is dead. He won't get loose in the night and shoot you and then go on to rape and kill some innocent woman while you feed the worms." The men looked at each other, nodding and smiling.

"To sum up, this is a tough job, but you will be paid well and will most likely become wealthy if you work hard and stay at it. So without further ado, I'd like to introduce our fearless leader John Thurgood Thomas."

JT stood up and put his hand on Gregor's shoulder. "Thank you, Gregor. But 'without further ado?' Are you kidding me?" he said in mock amazement.

The grouped laughed again. Gregor raised his hand. "Hey, I heard that in a speech once and I always wanted to use it!" he exclaimed with a wide grin.

JT smiled. "Okay, well here is my 'ado'. I support everything Mr. Nelson has said. And I want you all to understand this: HE IS THE BOSS, I am not. What Mr. Nelson says goes, without exception. Is that understood?"

B.J. sat forward. "We understand that, Mr. Thomas. None of us would be here if he wasn't leading this outfit. I've known him for over ten years, even partnered with him on a few jobs, and he is one of the finest men I have ever ridden with." The group broke into spontaneous applause as Gregor nearly blushed. "But I have one question—what do we call ourselves?"

Gregor stood up and put his arm on JT's shoulder. "I can answer that. We are the Thomas Agency, but you can call yourselves the 'Tommies' for short. Now go out and do the name justice! Drinks and supper are being served over at Emma's boarding house."

The men filed out, stopping to shake hands with their new employers. JT was the last one out looking out at the sky and thinking about his beloved Annabelle.

I wish she could have been here to see this, he thought, as he strode through the snow toward Emma's. As he mounted the steps, he could have sworn he heard sleigh bells in the distance. And he smiled.

Chapter Thirty-Eight

Tim Yates was watching his brother-in-law Phil cut hair in his tonsorial shop. Tim had to admit Phil was very good and his customers seemed to be pleased when he was finished. On the other hand, Tim had tried cutting Phil's hair and it was a disaster. The man looked like he was from another planet. Phil explained to each customer what had happened, and they all declined to have Tim cut their hair. That left Tim standing on the sidelines watching, wishing he could be outside or at least not watching hair drift down on his shoes. An opening at a local ranch had been filled before he applied for the job, and he'd never make any money cutting hair now. He was staying at the hotel, which would burn through the money he had received from Duvall in a few months.

JT Thomas opened the door, stomping the snow from his shoes and nodding at Tim and Phil. He sat down in a chair facing the windows. "What the hell happened to your head, Phil? Looks like you took on a grizzly and got the hell beaten out of you!" The other customer laughed.

Tim hung his head and Phil frowned. "I don't want to talk about it. Let's just say Timmy isn't cut out to be a barber."

Tim shot Phil a sharp look, tore off his apron, and stormed out into the cold. Phil frowned. "Darn, I shouldn't have said that. But he needs to be out and about, taking care of horses and such. He is a great guy, but hell, we all have our calling and cutting hair is not his! He'll be back, though—he forgot his hat and coat!"

Phil finished up with his customer and made a sweeping motion for JT to climb into the chair. JT sat, then pulled out his Colt and set it on his chest. Phil looked at him quizzically. "JT, are you going to shoot me if I mess up your hair?"

JT chuckled. "Naw, but there may well be a few drifters that haven't gotten the message about my reward being canceled." Phil nodded and swept the barber cape over the gun. "But if I end up looking like you, I just might wound you." And they both laughed.

Tim stepped back into the shop, shivering. He sat down and slipped on his coat as he looked at his brother-in-law. "Sorry, Phil. I know you're trying to help, but I just can't picture myself doing this for the rest of my life."

Phil nodded. "That's okay Tim, I understand. You need to be around horses. I know how you love them."

Tim snuggled into his coat and smiled. "Yeah, I do. I surely do."

JT looked over at the young Mr. Yates. "Tim, it so happens I may have an opportunity that you'll find attractive. How would you like to run a livery?"

Tim sat up straight. "Really? That would be great! But Buck's is the only livery in town, and he ain't about to move."

Phil finished cutting JT's hair and handed him a small mirror. JT looked at his new haircut and nodded as Phil swept the cape off. "Nice job, Phil. I guess I don't have to shoot you."

"Thank God! I've got a wife and baby to feed," Phil chuckled.

"Well then, Happy Holidays to you and your lovely family," JT said, paying Phil and giving him a generous tip.

He turned to Tim. "Tim, I'm going to talk to Buck for a bit. How about I meet you over at the Stevens Saloon in an hour? I'll buy you a holiday drink or two."

Tim grinned from ear to ear. "Why, that's mighty nice of you, Mr. Thomas."

≈ ≈ ≈ ≈ ≈

Duvall was living comfortably in his new town. He had cleaned up the drifters and made quite a bit of bounty money. Which was good, because when he wired Marcus Payne's lawyer in New York for more money he learned that Payne's assets were frozen.

Some of the outlaws were wanted alive, but Duvall gunned them down anyway. He hated paperwork, and the thought of feeding a prisoner three meals a day made him shudder. The town council members were not so enthused about this, and some were thinking about relieving him of his duties. But no one wanted to confront a man with a quick draw and such a short temper.

He was having an afternoon coffee as he sorted through the weekly mail. unrolling the new wanted posters that had been on his desk for over a week. The first was for a petty thief who had stuck up a mercantile shop, got away with seven dollars, and was wanted alive. The second was for a rapist and murderer who had killed four members of a family in their cabin outside of Greeley, Colorado, and the reward was $1,000. *That one would be worth my time,* he thought.

He spread out the next poster and spilled hot coffee in his lap as he jumped up. "God damn it!" he exclaimed, looking at a very good likeness of himself. "Fugitive Wanted," the poster read. "Accessory to murder. Attempted murder. Impersonating an officer." The list continued, and the blood drained from his face when he saw "$5,000 Reward" at the bottom.

He stood in shock for a minute, then turned and ran to the boarding house. After loading up his saddlebags and changing his pants, he left a twenty-dollar bill on the bed for Mary Ann. He looked around the room, then closed the door and strode quickly to the bank.

He went up to the teller's cage. "I'm closing my account," he said. "Cash me out."

"I'm sorry to hear that, Sheriff," the man said, as he checked the ledger and began pulling bills from the drawer. "Are you unhappy with the bank?"

"I'm unhappy with the whole damn situation. Now hurry your ass up!" Duvall growled.

As he turned to leave, he spotted the revoked reward poster for JT, and his memory of the dynamite jolted him. He stood riveted to the spot, his eyes burning a hole into the poster. He knew where to find his nemesis and he made up his mind in a New York heartbeat.

That man is the reason I'm in this mess. I'm going to kill that son of a bitch once and for all, reward or no reward!

≈ ≈ ≈ ≈ ≈

JT made his way through the snow to Buck's livery, sliding open the door and quickly closing it against the unseasonable cold. Buck was dressed warmly, since he had no stove or heat in the livery barn.

Buck looked up and grinned. "Hello, JT. What brings you out in this cold?"

JT sat down on a bale of hay. "Well, I wanted to chat with you."

Buck came out of the stall he was mucking out and sat down across from JT. "Okay, but before you do, I want to thank you for the supper. It was the best night I've had since my Martha passed. Your friends are very nice, and it was good to laugh with good folks."

JT smiled. "It was good of you to come. All my friends loved you, and Dawn and Emma think you are very handsome."

Buck blushed. "Well, you wanted to talk to me, so let's talk. But could you make it short? My helper is gone for the holidays and I'm doing twice the work."

JT leaned forward. "Buck, I'm moving to Arizona to start a ranch. It's going to be a big one. I'm going to build the house of my dreams and raise horses and cattle. But to do it, I am going to need help from people I trust."

"What a good idea! Some of my best times were spent on a ranch. The pay is never very good, but it's probably the best work in the world."

JT looked around. "Better than this?"

Buck laughed. "You mean shoveling horse shit? Oh, I like it most of the time, but there is something special about a roundup and a night shift on a trail drive. And the camaraderie is something special," he said, staring out into his past.

JT pulled a piece of hay out of the bale and began to chew on it. "Well, Buck, I'd like you to come with me. You'd be running the ranch as my right-hand man. I will pay you well, and you can live in the house with me until we build you a house on the grounds. I'll pay you $250 a month and a nice Christmas bonus if we are doing well. I will have a chef on the premises, and you are welcome to eat in the house, three squares a day. After five years, you pick the location and I'll carve out a piece of the ranch for you. I'll give you $5,000 in startup money, and you can start your own ranch." He grinned at Buck, who was standing wide-eyed. "So, what do you say?"

Buck stood up and picked up his pitchfork. "Well, just one hitch. What would I do with the livery? I've invested quite a bit of money in it, and it is finally doing well. I'll never get rich from it, but…"

JT spread his hands. "I'll buy it from you. Just name the price."

Buck looked around, dropped the pitchfork, and wiped his hands on his pants legs. He walked over and extended his hand. "You have got yourself a deal, Mr. Thomas!"

Chapter Thirty-Nine

J ean rolled over in her small bed and sighed as Ceros T. McGriff lit a cigar. "Well, honey bunch, I must say that was a good one," he leered. "You must like the holidays."

"I like having you all to myself," Jean purred. "How long is your wife going to be in St. Louis?"

The banker smiled. "Five glorious days," he said, leaning back and puffing on the cigar.

Jean got up and poured him another glass of whiskey. "I'll be right back," she whispered, then opened her door and stepped to head of the stairs. It was three in the morning, the saloon was empty, and the town was asleep. She returned to her room. "Ceros, I changed my mind. Let's go to your house. I'm guessing your bed is bigger than this little thing."

McGriff sat up, put his feet on the floor, and threw back his drink. "Now you're talking, honey bunch. Let's get dressed and head on over."

Jean dropped to her knees, bringing out a bag stuffed with bills and coins. "I can't leave this here," she said, handing the heavy bag over.

"Not to worry. We can stop at my bank, and I'll toss this in the safe. Then it's five days of jig jig!"

Jean smiled and gave him a kiss on his head. "Let's get going then."

It was bitter cold, and the moon was bright as they made their way into the bank. Ceros was too drunk to unlock the door, so Jean took the key from him. Once inside, she looked around the lobby, noting the moonlight streaming through the windows. "Let's get to your office, Ceros. It's too bright in here and I don't want anyone to see us," she murmured. He nodded and stumbled forward.

McGriff sat in his wheeled desk chair, winded from the trip from the saloon. Jean handed him her bag, and he scooted his chair over to the safe. He fumbled with the combination, then turned to Jean. "Honey bunch, I'm too drunk to open it. Let's leave it here for now."

Jean knelt down and whispered in his ear. "If you want jig jig, we need to open it. This may not be much to you, but it's my life savings. Just tell me the combination and we will get out of here." She gave him a long sweet kiss, sticking her tongue in his mouth and stroking his crotch.

"Aw, all right, honey bunch. It's three to the right, four to the left, one to the right, and one to the left."

Jean quickly opened the safe and put her bag inside. She pushed the door shut and twisted the lock back. "Let's go, lover," she said, as she took his arm and led the way.

The town was silent, bitterly cold and brilliantly lit by the moon. Once inside the banker's home, McGriff pointed the way upstairs. Jean opened the bedroom door and pulled back the sheets. She led the stumbling banker to his bed, undressed him, then bent over his lap and brought a smile to his face.

When she was done and the man was snoring drunkenly, Jean picked up a heavy pillow and put it over his face, pressing down with all her might. McGriff struggled a bit and his legs kicked randomly, but he was so thoroughly inebriated that his struggles were soon over. Jean waited a few minutes then took the pillow off, then pinched his nose shut and put her hand over his mouth for another few minutes to satisfy herself that he was truly dead.

She hung his clothes in his closet and considered finding his pajamas. But the thought of dressing a dead man made her shudder, so she tucked the sheets around him, hoping that whoever found him would think he died in his sleep. She took one last look at him before she left.

Well, at least he died happy.

≈≈≈≈≈

JT and Buck stood at the bar of the Stevens Saloon as Tim opened and closed the saloon doors quickly. The batwing doors were pushed to the side and the thick overnight doors were closed to fight the bitter cold. JT picked up his bottle of Scotch and motioned Tim over to a table in the corner, close to one of the stoves. They all sat down, and Buck reached out to shake Tim's hand. "Good to see you Tim, and congratulations."

JT grinned and Tim frowned. "It's good to see you too, Buck, but I've given up on cutting hair, so congratulations aren't really necessary," he grumbled. Buck laughed as JT poured a round of Scotch.

"Tim, I have a story for you," JT said. "I'm moving to Arizona and I'm taking Buck with me. So I'm buying his livery and I'm going to need someone to manage it for me. I'm thinking if that person sticks around for three years, I'll give him 50% ownership. I'll also pay him $100 a month and three squares at the hotel café or Emma's boarding house. Buck's helper stays too."

Tim nodded and took a long swallow of Scotch. "That sounds like a pretty darn good deal, but what does it have to do with me, Mr. Thomas? You're not forgetting how we met, are you?"

JT chuckled. "No, I'm not forgetting, but I believe you made a young man's mistake and fell in with the wrong people."

Tim hung his head and nodded. "Thanks for being so understanding, Mr. Thomas. But just so I understand, are you making me this incredibly generous offer?"

JT smiled and nodded. "That is right, Tim. So, what do you say?"

Tim's eyes lit up. "Are you kidding? I'm your man!" The men smiled, shook hands, and clinked their glasses together.

"Mr. Thomas, I got to tell you that you are a mighty good egg," Tim said, beaming.

≈ ≈ ≈ ≈ ≈

Jean opened the bank doors and locked them behind her. The lobby was still brilliantly lit as she made her way to Ceros' office. She quickly opened the safe, humming "Three, four, one, and IN!" The safe was so loaded she had a difficult time making a decision. She loved the gold as it gleamed in the moonlight, but since she didn't have her brother to help her carry such a heavy load she sighed and decided to leave where it was. However, there were stacks and stacks of bills that Jean quickly stuffed into a bank bag, turning it inside out so the bank logo was not visible. Behind the bills, she discovered a small bag filled with diamonds. She smiled and stuffed it in her coat, then closed the safe and left the office, locking the door behind her. Not seeing a rear exit, she made her way through the brilliantly lit lobby. On the way out, she spotted a large bulletin board and froze in her spot.

JT Thomas's image stared out at her from an "All is forgiven" poster. JT Thomas—the killer of her brother Cain. Was he still alive? She thought she had killed him in his beloved cave. But why would a bank have this poster in the lobby if he were truly dead? She needed to think about this. In the meantime, she was going to buy a place she'd seen for sale on a lake outside of Ashcroft, with the intention of rebuilding her beloved cabin. It would be a good place to plot revenge. "God damn JT Thomas," she growled.

Chapter Forty

JT met with Emma, Gregor, Dawn, and DeWitt in Emma's café and informed his friends of his offers to Buck and Tim Yates. They were all excited, though sorry at the prospect of JT heading to Arizona.

Gregor stood up and rapped on his glass with his spoon. "Thank you all for coming. Emma and I are very excited about the opening tomorrow, and we wanted to thank you all for everything you've done to help us make it happen."

"Hear, hear," DeWitt boomed out and the table laughed.

"However, I have another announcement to make. Emma and I are getting married!" he said, kissing and hugging her.

Emma stood with a glowing smile on her face, showing her friends a gleaming diamond ring on her finger. Everyone applauded and expressed their delight at the news. "I want to especially thank JT for his wonderful generosity," Emma said, discretely glancing at the diamond.

JT smiled and nodded as dinner arrived. "Well then, let's dig in!" Gregor said, grinning. The friends toasted and had a wonderful meal of pheasant, glazed carrots, and fried potatoes, followed by a dessert of peach cobbler and the doctor's Grand Marnier.

Afterward, Emma called out her new chefs. "These ladies are known as the best cooks in town, so I offered them a promotion to chef in the café. What do you think?" The group gave the women congratulations and applause, which they accepted gratefully before returning to the kitchen.

DeWitt stood up. "Well, Dawn and I also have an announcement!" he said, smiling widely as Dawn stood up and linked her arm with his. "Dawn has honored me by accepting my proposal of marriage. We have set the date for Christmas. I will have a ring by then." He grinned slyly. "Or sooner, if JT might want to donate to our cause!'

The friends exploded in laughter, and JT nodded affirmatively. "I would be delighted and honored to. Doctor, would you like to pick out the diamond or would Dawn like to?"

DeWitt began to reply, but Dawn put her hand on his arm. "I'll be choosing, thank you very much! Thank you, thank you!" she exclaimed.

"Hear, hear," DeWitt said with a wide grin, then sat down and sipped his orange liqueur.

≈≈≈≈≈

As they were leaving the café, Gregor took JT aside and asked, "Any news about Xavier Duvall's whereabouts these days?"

E. Alan Fleischauer

JT shrugged and replied, "No one knows, and no one really cares at the moment."

Chapter Forty-One

Christmas came sooner than anyone wanted, as the last month had been spent preparing for the weddings and sending out invitations. Gregor and Emma had decided to join the good doctor and Dawn with a Christmas wedding and the anxiety was at an all-time peak. Guests had arrived the week before, and every available room in town was full to capacity. From New York came Annabelle's daughter Maddy and old friend Mrs. C., who added to the excitement by announcing that she and her beau Raphael were also going to be married on Christmas Day. Everyone thought a triple wedding was a splendid idea.

Maddy and JT spent a quiet evening in the hotel café catching up on things and talking about Annabelle. Gregor assigned Brett Newman to guard and chauffeur Maddy around town, and she confided to Dawn how impressed she was with Steffon. She was reluctant to use his nickname Stiff, since it reminded her of a corpse. "He is SOOO handsome with his beautiful red hair," she said, touching her own red hair. Dawn broadcast Maddy's feelings to anyone who would listen, often while showing off her new engagement ring.

JT was asked to be best man at all three weddings and readily agreed, pulling out Annabelle's favorite suit for the occasion.

Christmas morning arrived with a wonderful break in the weather. It was as if God was honoring the happy couples. The church was filled for a four o'clock ceremony, and the guests packed the pews. The grade school choir was doing an encore performance from the morning services. Buck and local friends of Gregor and DeWitt served as groomsmen. Emma and Dawn had only a few bridesmaids since her chefs and best friends were busy preparing a scrumptious reception meal to be served in the church basement.

Tim Yates' sister Sarah played the organ as the three couples walked down the aisle side by side. The minister, a brown-haired middle-aged man with piercing green eyes led the ceremony, singing in a beautiful baritone.

As the couples reached the altar, the minister stood in front of the congregation and began reciting the vows. He addressed the room. "If anyone objects to these marriages, speak up now or forever hold your peace."

The room was silent, and as he was about to continue a man stepped out from the rear of the church. He made his way up the center aisle, removing his hat and looking directly at JT.

"I object," bellowed Xavier Duvall. "I object to JT Thomas being alive, and I will meet him out in the street once you're done with this nonsense." He replaced his hat, turned, and walked out the door.

The anxious wedding participants and congregants began milling about, murmuring. The minister was taken aback, as nothing like this had ever happened to him before. It was JT who held his hand up, signaling for quiet. "I am very sorry about that. Let us resume the ceremony, and I will take care of this." He signaled to Stiff and Will to follow Duvall out into the street and stand guard in case he decided to change his mind and reenter the church.

JT looked at the Minister. "Please proceed," he stated firmly.

Finally, the rings were exchanged, the brides were kissed, and the minister, having regained his composure, shouted out, "I now pronounce you man and wife, times three!" The church members broke into applause, then turned and stared at JT. "I will be right back," he said, as he made his way down the aisle to the doors.

Duvall was leaning on a corral post and staring at JT with an evil smile. He pushed away from the fence and began to remove his hammer strap.

In a flash, something red snarled and leaped off the portico of the building the corral was attached to. JT recognized it as his guardian angel, Red. The cougar landed on Duvall's chest, knocking him to the ground. Stiff and Will began to raise their weapons, but JT signaled for them to stop.

Duvall's struggles were weakening as the big cat dragged him by the throat, shaking her head and moving quickly out of sight behind the building. JT turned to look at Gregor and the rest of the wedding entourage, which had gathered behind him.

"Thank you, Annabelle," JT whispered, as he heard sleigh bells in the distance. "And Merry Christmas!"

Acknowledgements

First and foremost, I thank my dear wife Paula. Having re-
tired after forty years of nursing, she continues to help me
edit my novels, gives me sage advice on what to leave in and,
more importantly, what to leave out – especially if I have
crossed over her feminine "don't go there" line.

Ken Schubert, my primary editor, deserves a lot of credit
for this second novel. I was on a writer's roll and sped right
into my third book, *Kidnapped*, thus dumping *Hunted* on Ken
with little or no direction. As usual, he did an excellent job
of filling in the cracks.

Many of you who read *Rescued* wanted a happier ending, so
the second edition addresses that, to a certain degree. I think
you will be pleased with the change.

Finally, I'm pleased that you bought this book and used your
valuable time to read it. If you liked it, then please leave a
nice review on Amazon. If you didn't, well, I don't know
what to tell you. Ha.

Anyway, I really do hope you enjoyed reading *Hunted* as
much as I did writing it!

Peace,

E. Alan Fleischauer

About the Author

E. Alan Fleischauer is a certified financial planner, an active member of numerous non-profit organizations, and a rock 'n' roll drummer. He lives west of the Mississippi River, an easy ride to his Wisconsin cabin.

COMING SOON

From Kidnapped, book three in the JT Thomas saga.

Brett took a drink and looked across the table at Dawn. "I followed Muddy a few miles down the stage trail. It looked like she met up with someone and rode with him for a bit. But then the rain hit and I lost their tracks."

Dawn shook her head at the distraught young man. "That's not good news. JT thinks of Maddy as his own daughter and would kill to protect her."

"Don't you think I know that? It was my job to look after her, and now she's gone."

"Well, what do you think happened?"

Brett paused for a moment, then looked Dawn in the eye. "I think she was kidnapped."